The Jasper ___
Invi___
Some Old-Fashioned Fun
as We Welcome Back Our Hometown Heroes for
an Old Timers' Baseball Game...
Montana Style!

There's nothing like baseball in Montana.
Is it the fresh mountain air? The cowboy mentality?
No one knows for certain. But it's no wonder the
Jasper Gulch Old Timers have captured our hearts!

And no two hearts could be more entwined than
Livvie Franklin's and Jack McGuire's. Though it's been
eight years since these former high school sweethearts
have laid eyes on each other, something tells us Livvie
has never gotten over her Jasper Gulch all-star.
Can the centennial celebration help them turn back time?
Join us in the bleachers as we root them on!

* * *

Big Sky Centennial:
A small town rich in history...and love.

Her Montana Cowboy by Valerie Hansen—*July 2014*
His Montana Sweetheart by Ruth Logan Herne—*August 2014*
Her Montana Twins by Carolyne Aarsen—*September 2014*
His Montana Bride by Brenda Minton—*October 2014*
His Montana Homecoming by Jenna Mindel—*November 2014*
Her Montana Christmas by Arlene James—*December 2014*

Books by Ruth Logan Herne

Love Inspired

Winter's End
Waiting Out the Storm
Made to Order Family
*Reunited Hearts
*Small-Town Hearts
*Mended Hearts
*Yuletide Hearts
*A Family to Cherish
*His Mistletoe Family
†The Lawman's Second Chance
†Falling for the Lawman
†The Lawman's Holiday Wish
†Loving the Lawman
His Montana Sweetheart

*Men of Allegany County
†Kirkwood Lake

RUTH LOGAN HERNE

Born into poverty, Ruth puts great stock in one of her favorite Ben Franklinisms: "Having been poor is no shame. Being ashamed of it is." With God-given appreciation for the amazing opportunities abounding in our land, Ruth finds simple gifts in the everyday blessings of smudge-faced small children, bright flowers, freshly baked goods, good friends, family, puppies and higher education. She believes a good woman should never fear dirt, snakes or spiders, all of which like to infest her aged farmhouse, necessitating a good pair of tongs for extracting the snakes, a flat-bottomed shoe for the spiders, and for the dirt...

Simply put, she's learned that some things aren't worth fretting about! If you laugh in the face of dust and love to talk about God, men, romance, great shoes and wonderful food, feel free to contact Ruth through her website, www.ruthloganherne.com.

His Montana Sweetheart

Ruth Logan Herne

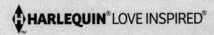

Special thanks and acknowledgment to Ruth Logan Herne for her contribution to the Big Sky Centennial miniseries.

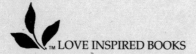

PLEASE RECYCLE · THIS PRODUCT IS RECYCLABLE ·

Recycling programs
for this product may
not exist in your area.

LOVE INSPIRED BOOKS

ISBN-13: 978-0-373-81780-1

HIS MONTANA SWEETHEART

Copyright © 2014 by Harlequin S.A.

www.Harlequin.com

Printed in U.S.A.

For now we see through a glass, darkly; but then face to face: now I know in part; but then shall I know even as also I am known.

—1 Corinthians 13:12

To my beloved father-in-law, Floyd "Sonny" Blodgett, a gentle man of few words and a loving heart. Dad suffered through the years of Alzheimer's slow decline with his family surrounding him. Dad, your example of handling whatever came your way has passed on through multiple generations. God truly blessed us with your kind, quiet presence. May you rest in the peace and light of God's eternal love.

Chapter One

Of all the town meetings, in all the world...

The altered line from *Casablanca* knotted Livvie Franklin's heart.

Jack. Here. Now.

She drew a breath that stuck square in her throat.

Tall. Still lanky, but with a shoulder breadth that made folks take notice, and from the appreciative glances of the single women in the room—and a couple of older mothers, too—she wasn't the only one who had noticed.

Green eyes. Brown hair, shaggy, in need of a cut, but she understood the rigors of ranching, and Jack had lost his mother a few years before. Now he and his dad had house chores on top of everything else in their short Big Sky growing season.

She knew she'd run into him sooner or later. In a town the size of Jasper Gulch no one stayed hidden forever.

But she'd dismissed the possibility at a council

meeting about the Old-timers' Baseball Game. Jack had shied away from all things baseball since he blew his arm out over eight years before. He decided then to shrug off ball-playing and his girl—*her*—as anathema.

So be it.

She'd slip out the back, she decided, but Olivia had forgotten the force of the locals. As soon as the small gathered crowd saw Jack—

The same folks who'd been greeting her since she came into town a few days before—

Heads swerved from Jack to her, their looks expectant.

Jack turned, following the track of their collective attention. He stopped. Stared. His gaze, always so open and trusting for the years they dated, was more somber. Surprise widened his eyes, and the saltwater green brightened.

He moved her way, preventing her escape, forcing a confrontation she didn't want. As he drew closer, with pretty much the entire group focused on this unplanned reunion of high school sweethearts gone amok, she forced herself to engage in a moment of self-honesty.

She *did* want to see him. She'd been hoping to see him. And she'd made sure she looked good before she left the house each day this week, just in case.

"Livvie."

"Jack."

For the life of her, the one word was all she could manage, looking up—way up—into the eyes she'd known and trusted for so long. Her Jack...

Then. Not now. She hauled in a breath and stuck out her hand. "Good to see you, although I'm surprised. I was pretty sure you'd stayed away from anything to do with baseball since college."

His expression confirmed her assumption, but his words surprised her. "Adam's little sister shamed me into it. I'm still wondering how to get even with her, but she's gone and gotten herself a cowboy fiancé and it would be too bad to burst their little bubble of happiness. Although the ride into town gave me time to ponder some creative options. He's in pretty good shape, though, so why tempt fate?"

Half hermit, Livvie's mother had said. *Keeps to himself. No one sees too much of him or his father these days.*

Change and grief. Livvie knew the reality of that firsthand but quelled her urge to sympathize with a dose of reality.

She'd loved Jack once. He'd broken her heart. Squaring her shoulders, she nodded toward the front. "I think they're getting things under way."

Resignation marked his gaze. For her? For the situation? The meeting?

She had no idea, but Livvie Franklin had vowed one thing on her long drive back to Jasper Gulch to help organize a town history for the ongoing Jasper

Gulch centennial festivities. The trip back home had been rife with self-appraisal. And the timing? Imperfectly perfect as she nursed the wounds of an unexpected divorce.

Jack McGuire was off-limits. She'd placed him in the high-risk category eight years before and there he'd stay, no matter how handsome he was, or how his eyes gazed straight into hers as though drinking in the vision.

She'd save her romantic notions for Jane Austen and history, a perfect coupling. Modern romance?

She'd finally figured out it was nothing to write home about.

Broadsided by the petite, blue-eyed blonde that had won his heart over a decade before. He stood before the board, offering what he hoped was a coherent report on the old-timers' game, but he couldn't wrap his head around baseball right now. Not with Livvie twenty feet to his left.

Why was she here? Were her parents okay? Was she?

Questions bombarded him from within and without, and he wasn't sorry when his elderly friend Rusty Zidek chimed in a time or two to clear matters up.

Were they gathering players?

Yes.

Were player shirts ordered for both teams?

They would be this week.

Had they invited Hutch Garrison, the current Jasper Gulch baseball success story, a newly signed outfielder for the Colorado Rockies?

Yes, but he hadn't been able to confirm his presence yet.

By the end of the back-and-forth, the board seemed satisfied with how things stood. Jack needed to hear from more players, but they had weeks to straighten things out, and a pledge from some guys in Bozeman to fill in if necessary. That bit of news made the council give a collective sigh of relief.

The mayor tipped the central microphone toward himself. "Jack, I'm speaking for the entire board when I say we're grateful you took this on when Wes got sick."

Wes Middleton, the previous chair of the Old-timers' Committee, had unexpectedly needed bypass surgery. Jack met the mayor's gaze frankly and replied, "I believe 'railroaded' by your youngest daughter would be a more apt term, sir. Seems the apple didn't fall too far from the tree in this case."

Mayor Shaw's gaze glinted with humor and something else. Regret? Maybe. But the look disappeared before Jack was sure he read it correctly. "Her mother's powers of persuasion, actually. You know how it is, Jack."

He didn't, not really, because he'd run cold and hard from anything to do with long-term relationships for years. Maybe he wasn't meant to settle down, settle in. Maybe—

A glimpse of wavy, layered blond hair to his left put his heart in pause mode. He'd blown it once, the only relationship that mattered. He'd tossed her overboard in a groundswell of self-pity and anger. Like Scrooge in the famous Dickens story, he might have ruined his one and only chance at love eight years before, but he had his ranch. And his father. And—

The appreciation list cut short right there because he'd already summed things up and felt the lack to his core. He drew a breath and nodded to the mayor, raised the few sheets of loose-leaf paper he'd brought and swept the board a glance that included Rusty. "We'll have it running smooth by game day."

He ignored the bemused look Rusty aimed his way, because Rusty was the only person who knew how little he had really done. The board nodded and moved on to the next item as Jack turned to say goodbye to Olivia.

Gone.

He scanned the room quickly.

No Olivia.

He headed toward the backdoor quicker than necessary, and when he stepped through and saw her perched on the brick wall alongside the steps, his heart did a rapid thump of gratitude, a reaction he didn't deserve and couldn't pursue. But for that one instant, a decades-old feeling power-rushed him, the way it used to every time he saw her. When she shifted her attention his way at the sound of the door, however, her gaze bordered on polite and distant, and that realization settled his pulse in quick order. "I thought you left."

"I am leaving, but I wanted to jot down a few names, and if I waited to do it at home I'd forget half."

"With your brains?" He scoffed and moved closer. "Not gonna happen. Are you here to visit? And why are you writing down random names? Did you drive in?"

She closed the electronic tablet and stood as she addressed his questions in order. "I'm in town to help put together a biographical history as part of the centennial. If my research goes well, my information will be ready by the time they open the new Jasper Gulch historical museum in December. I came into town tonight because I thought some of the old-timers coming in for the game could help fill in some time-line gaps I'm seeing." She didn't add that she assumed Wes Middleton was in charge of the game, and that if she'd known Jack was involved, she'd have shied away, but her expression made that clear.

"The car question?" She turned her gaze toward a red compact angled into a parking slot up the road. "I figured it would be dark by the time the meeting was done, or at least by the time I made it home, and walking the two-lane at dusk is stupid."

It was. Sun glare blurred the horizon and the road at dawn and dusk. She'd made a smart choice, but that was no big surprise. Her brilliance had earned her a prestigious scholarship to Stanford, while he'd been playing ball five hours south at UCLA. A long-distance relationship that worked until…

He cut that thought short by hooking a thumb south. "You got time to walk, Liv? Catch up? Somewhere that every citizen of Jasper Gulch isn't watching?"

Oh, she had time, all right. Nothing but time. And he was right about the citizenry because she'd been fielding questions about her marital status and Jack's single-guy life for the past seven days, as if one plus one should naturally equal two.

They didn't, of course. Not all equations worked out in mathematical precision, especially with human quotients.

But did she have the moxie to maintain polite distance from Jack McGuire, her first love? She hesitated, knowing she was vulnerable, lost in the kicked-up dust of a three-year marriage gone bad the year before.

She'd wanted a family.

Her husband had wanted a divorce. Since the two were at distinct odds, he had hightailed it out of their marriage and into the arms of a woman he'd met eighteen months before, a woman he'd married and had a baby with not long after the ink dried on the divorce decree. Which meant for well over a year Billy Margulies had been living a lie. She wasn't sure which hurt more—his lie or the fact that she fell for his act the entire time.

Jack tipped his gaze down, and that sweet expression, hinting question and tinged with humor, made her decision hard and easy. "Yes. I've got time for a walk. A quick one."

He rocked back on his heels and dipped his chin, total cowboy. He didn't reach for her hand as she slipped her iPad into the tooled-leather Western bag at her side, but he looked as if he wanted to hold her hand, and that evoked a wave of sweet memories best kept at bay.

Here in Jasper Gulch, where every storefront and street held a memory?

Keeping those thoughts in their place would be tough to do.

Tongue-tied.

Jack headed toward the old bridge, trudging the worn path with Olivia as he'd done so often in the past. But things were different now. Knowing that, understanding the ensuing years had gone downstream swift as minnows from the Big Timber fish hatchery, he knew nothing would negate the past, but he'd hurt this girl—*woman,* he corrected himself—and fate or God had put her in his path tonight. Maybe he could make amends.

"I hated you for a long time."

Jack quickly downscaled amends to initial-apology status. Amends would take longer. Like maybe forever. Or never. He winced inside because talking wasn't his strong point, and waded into the waters of repentance with "guilty as charged" stamped on his forehead. "You had reason to."

She acknowledged that with a questioning look. "Yes and no."

"My vote is yes because I threw a hissy fit about my injury, dumped you, chased off after a career I ended up not liking, then came back home with my tail tucked between my legs like a naughty pup."

"Your mother's illness brought you back," she corrected him. "And you did the right thing. But was it the job you hated, or the city?" She asked the question without looking at him, skimming right over the whole part where he admitted to dumping her. Breaking her heart.

Unless he hadn't broken her heart.

That thought rankled enough to have him clap a hand to the nape of his neck.

And then a surge of instant guilt sprouted because the idea she might not have been all that heartbroken irked him. What kind of man was he?

Shallow, self-absorbed, inwardly focused, take your pick, advised his conscience.

He preferred God-fearing, upright and responsible, but the past year had nudged his conscience into a more accurate appraisal. Ignoring the internal stab, he pondered her question as they approached the creek bank above the rapids. "Eventually I grew to hate both," he admitted. "I actually didn't mind the city at first. It was vibrant. Different. Full of life."

"Chicago's crazy fun," Olivia offered, and the way she said it, as if she'd been there, stopped him in his tracks.

"How do you know that?"

"I completed my studies on East Fifty-ninth Street in the university's Social Sciences Division."

Irked spiraled to flat-out irritated in a heartbeat. "You did your grad work at the University of Chicago? And never contacted me?"

This time she faced him, and the look she gave him, a mix of resignation and old hurt, put him flat in his place, just where he belonged. "You didn't want me, Jack. You made that clear. I wouldn't have even known you were there except that my parents mentioned it. But that didn't mean I shouldn't pursue my master's degree at one of the best schools in the country. So I did."

The thought of Livvie in Chicago all that time, while he was slogging away in investment banking, made his head spin. She'd known where he was, had proximity to him and didn't make contact.

You told her not to, scolded the internal voice

again. *Didn't your mother tell you not to say things you didn't mean?*

She had, Jack knew. Back in kindergarten. He should have listened better.

"Because while the city was okay for a while, a means to an end," Livvie continued in an easy voice, "I was glad to get out of there. Come back to Big Sky country." She spread her hands out, leaned back and watched the encroaching night. "We used to count the stars at night, Jack. When they came out. Remember that?"

Oh, he remembered, all right. They'd look skyward and watch each star appear, summer, winter, spring and fall, each season offering its own array, a blend of favorites. Until they'd become distracted by other things. Sweet things.

A sigh welled from somewhere deep within him, a quiet blooming of what could have been. "I remember."

They stared upward, side by side, watching the sunset fade to streaks of lilac and gray. Town lights began to appear north of the bridge, winking on earlier now that it was August. "How long are you here?"

She faltered. "I'm not sure."

He turned to face her, puzzled.

"I'm between lives right now."

He raised an eyebrow, waiting for her to continue. She did, after drawn-out seconds, but didn't look at him. She kept her gaze up and out, watching the tree shadows darken and dim.

"I was married."

He'd heard she'd gotten married several years ago, but the "was" surprised him. He dropped his gaze to her left hand. No ring. No tan line that said a ring had been there this summer. A flicker that might be hope stirred in his chest, but entertaining those notions would get him nothing but trouble, so he blamed the strange feeling on the half-finished sandwich he'd wolfed down on the drive in.

You've eaten fast plenty of times before this, and been fine. Just fine.

The reminder made him take a half step forward, just close enough to inhale the scent of sweet vanilla on her hair, her skin.

He shouldn't. He knew that. He knew it even as his hand reached for her hand, the left one bearing no man's ring, and that touch, the press of his fingers on hers, made the tiny flicker inside brighten just a little. "What happened?"

"A really cute office assistant who doesn't spend all her time with her head in books. Or so I was told."

A curl of anger poised alongside the other feelings Jack worked to contain. The look on her face said wrath was unneeded, but old-fashioned sympathy? He squeezed the hand that felt so familiar—and so good. "The guy's a jerk."

She didn't agree. Did that mean she still had feelings for her ex-husband? That she still loved him?

Well, why not? It had been over eight years since Jack cut Olivia loose.

Seeing her raised a wealth of memories. High school dances. Trips to the river. Hiking. Fishing.

Kissing.

She'd been his first date. His first kiss. His first love.

Then he'd blown it in a fit of infantile "why me?" temper.

And here she was, in Jasper Gulch, standing by his side on the worn, neglected bridge over Beaver Creek, and she was in love with someone else. He deserved no more, but for just a second he wished for more.

"Do you have kids?"

She shook her head, and he thought her eyes went moist, but the old-style lanterns at either end of the bridge cast her gaze in silhouette. "No kids." She turned his way. "How about you? Married? Kids?"

He dropped her hand and shook his head. "Nope."

"And you worked in the city for years," she continued, looking up at him, straight at him, as if trying to decipher who he was from who he'd been way back then. "But didn't go back after—"

"Losing my mother." He stared into the night, wondering why talking with Livvie Franklin loosened his tongue. "You know, it's strange, when someone's so sick, Liv. You help, you care for them, you do all the little things you know are right, you try to be the good person, and no matter how sick they are, no matter how long it takes, when they're gone, you still have this feeling like you didn't do enough. Never enough."

"And that would be the last thing your mother would want you to feel," countered Livvie. "She loved you, Jack. She'd never want you to beat yourself up over her death, especially when you already tend to beat yourself up over things. Your mother knew that."

She leaned against the bridge, but Jack pulled her forward. "I don't trust these supports. The bridge has been let go for too long, and I'm not about to let you be the second Jasper Gulch tragedy."

"Not fixing the bridge is a foolish lack of tribute to an old accident," she replied. "I'm sure Lucy Shaw would be appalled to think it, if she'd lived." She pulled her arm free with a speed that warned him off, and rightfully so, he supposed.

But being there? On the bridge they'd walked across so often as a young couple? The bridge that marked so much of their town's history?

The surroundings, the trees, the thin-lit night and the sound of rushing water below made him feel as if anything was possible, and he hadn't felt that way in a very long time. But here, with her?

He did. And it felt good.

Chapter Two

It took every ounce of strength for Olivia to keep her cool when Jack took her hand, but she did it.

And when he talked about his mother's death, about losing Mary Beth McGuire to cancer three years before, she longed to reach out. Hug him. And maybe never let go.

Residual nonsense from long ago, don't you dare. You prepared for this possibility the whole drive down. Stay tough. Stay strong. Maintain a distance at all costs and, whatever you do, Do Not Stare Into Those Amazing Green Eyes.

Olivia's gut recognized the sensibility of the mental tirade, but there was a spot around her heart, a fairly big spot, that longed to make everything right for Jack McGuire. Which meant she was a pushover for that cleft chin and crooked smile, even after all this time. She erected an internal Danger Zone sign and kept her voice calm, her face serene, but inside?

She wanted answers. She wanted love. She wanted something functional out of the past eight years of study, work, marriage and building a home.

And here she was, jobless, homeless, divorced and sleeping in her old room in her parents' house, as dysfunctional as you could get. She'd become the statistic she abhorred, the failure-to-launch young adult who crept back to the nest. How had this happened?

The sweet rhythmic toll of a bell interrupted her funk.

She turned, surprised, and Jack pointed northwest. "First Monday prayer service at the church." When she frowned, he continued, "Our new pastor started this. It's an evening prayer service to mark the first Monday of each month. A call to worship. Ethan says he wants folks to pause and think about things now and again, and there's nothing like an evening prayer service to do that." He directed his gaze back to town in a silent invitation to retrace their steps, then added, "It's kind of nice, though I've only been to one so far."

The thought of Monday-night church seemed odd enough, but the idea of Jack leaving the ranch, getting cleaned up and rolling into town for a prayer service surprised her even more. Work had always come first on the Double M. School. Baseball. The ranch. Chores. Church had fallen well down the list of Jack McGuire priorities, but the look on his face said that might have changed.

She fell into step beside him, thoughtful, letting the recorded bells' chime call them back to Main Street. They drew near to the corner as the bell went silent. An awkward quiet rose around them until Jack motioned west toward the quaint stone-and-wood church. "Would you like to go? We wouldn't be all that late."

She wouldn't, no, but she didn't know how to say that and not sound like a jerk. She hemmed and hawed, and let Jack draw his own conclusions.

He did. Quickly. He gave her a glimpse of that endearing smile, then doffed his hat, cowboy to the core. "Nice seeing you, Liv."

"Nice, yes. You, too, Jack."

He watched as she climbed into her car, ever the gentleman, except when he tossed her aside like yesterday's news.

And then he watched as she drove away, his gaze following her until she turned left on River Road and headed home.

Did he turn and go to the church service? She had no idea and wasn't sure she cared to know, because she used to pray all the time. About life, about love, about Jack, her family, her sister, her dog. Her latest prayers had centered on her marriage and the family she'd longed to have, a couple of cute kids running around, wreaking havoc, making her smile.

She'd lost Jack, her sister had moved away years before, the dog had passed on while she was married to Billy and she'd watched her marriage and dreams of a family go up in a puff of divorce-petition smoke.

So if there was a God…? If He existed some-where other than the pages of an often-interpreted book? She hadn't seen much evidence of it, and right now didn't care to search anymore.

She'd count her blessings, the human ones, and move on, heart guarded, because fewer people got hurt that way. Mainly her.

Bright windows welcomed her back to her par-ents' home on Old Trail Road. The house, set into the edge of a wooded grove, looked happy and natural, at peace with its surroundings. The front screen door slapped shut as she exited the car, and the scent of fresh-baked cookies hit the evening air like a gift. "You baked? In this heat?"

Her mother's smile said yes as she nodded to-ward the second porch rocker. "I figured evening time would be fine. We've got fans in the bedrooms and the cool night air will chase off the oven's heat by morning."

"True enough. I know it's the beginning of Au-gust, but the thick morning dew says fall isn't far off."

"I won't wish the summer away," her mother re-plied. "They're too scant here, and after last win-ter's wrath, I've no desire to see snow for a while. And while fall was always my favorite season in

Michigan, here in Montana it comes and goes too fast. And the colors aren't the same."

"I noticed that when I went to visit Grandma and Grandpa in Detroit a few years back." Liv settled into the rocker, and let the easy motion ease the tiredness from her back, her shoulders. "Have you heard from them this week?"

"I call Mom every night, actually."

Liv turned, sensing trouble, because fear or concern would be the only reason her mother and grandmother would be in constant contact. "Is Grandpa okay?" Her mother's expression said he wasn't. "Tell me, Mom. What's going on?"

"We think it's Alzheimer's."

The possibility of her grandfather succumbing to the mind-numbing illness chilled Livvie. She leaned forward. "You think it is? Or you know it?"

Jane Franklin pursed her mouth and shrugged. "It's hard to tell in the beginning stages because everyone forgets things from time to time, but for Grandpa it's been over a year of little things building up."

"Over a year?" Liv sat straight up in the chair. "And you haven't said anything?"

"Your grandmother was adamant about not making a big deal if it was nothing more than a phase. But it looks like it's the real deal, and we can't leave Grandma to care for him alone. She hates the idea of coming to Montana, but their neighborhood isn't like it used to be, and a forgetful old man makes an easy target on the streets."

Mixed emotions swept Olivia.

Her grandparents loved Detroit. They'd been a big part of their local church; they'd known every family, every elder, every kid in their congregation for decades. The butcher on the corner was her grandfather's best friend, the local bakery was run by a neighbor's daughter, and the small diner up the road was owned by her aunt's godparents. Tucked between the city and the suburbs, their neighborhood had survived when others failed, but Olivia had seen the beginnings of decay when she'd visited five years ago.

Guilt swept her. Why was there five years between visits? She hadn't been that busy, not busy enough to ignore her grandparents. But that's exactly what she'd done, believing things would go on forever.

Right, her brain chided. *How's that whole forever thing working out for you?* She shushed the internal stab and faced her mother. "What's the plan?"

"Dad and I are spending next week there. We're taking the car instead of the SUV because Grandma has a harder time climbing into a taller vehicle. And I think…" She paused, then firmed her gaze and her stance in the chair, "I hope we'll be bringing them back here. That way we can all help each other."

"Change scares folks."

Her mother acknowledged that with a dip of her chin.

"But I'd rather have them cranky for a while than hurt. Or alone. Or fearful in their own house."

"Exactly the case, but now I have to convince my mother of that. Dad's kind of oblivious to the whole thing. But Mom?" The look she sent Olivia said she was preparing for battle. "She'll be tough to convince."

"Which is where I come in." Dave Franklin approached the porch from his workshop in the garage. "I was able to sweet-talk the daughter into moving west. I think I'll do just fine with the mother."

Her parents exchanged smiles, a tangible warmth of time, love and faith, the kind of married-forever look Livvie had longed for.

"I'm okay with you taking the helm," Jane declared. "My mother hates to think her kids are bossing her around—"

Liv sent a mock-guilty look her mother's way, because hadn't she scolded her mother that very morning for leaving fruit on the counter, a breeding ground for dozens of fruit flies?

Her mother's smile said the fruit was still on the counter because refrigeration broke down the sugar content or some such nonsense. Three bossy women in one house?

That scenario meant Liv better figure out where

she was going and what she was doing sooner rather than later. But for now— "Dad's got a touch, that's for sure. I'll make certain the downstairs bedroom is clean."

"A few prayers would be a nice addition," her father mused. "I think Grandma's had a lot on her plate, and the thought of closing up the house, selling things, or sorting through and giving them away, weighs on her."

"A daunting task," Jane agreed. "But we can help while we're there. And if we bring them here, I think your aunt Kathy would step in and oversee the real estate sale. She's closest." Jane turned back to Liv. "I'm sorry we're ducking out on you your second week back, but you'll be busy with your historical research and the centennial stuff, so it should be fine. Right?"

Talk about embarrassing. To have a mother coddling a thirty-year-old daughter in the very nest she was born in?

Liv bit back a growl of self-contempt and nodded. "I'm knee-deep in research now, and actually loving it. The Lewis and Clark influence on this part of the country, the early settlers east of here, the problems that brought the Shaw and Massey families across the state to settle in the gulch? There's some truth-is-stranger-than-fiction stuff in those old stories. So I'm fine, I'll take care of everything here—"

"Including Tabby."

The overweight cat shifted on the porch glider. He yawned, stretched and settled back into slumber on the woven floral cushion, a purr of contentment lulling the old boy back to sleep.

"I'm putting him on an exercise regimen the minute you're gone," Liv confirmed, but she softened the order by reaching out and stroking the gray-striped cat's head. "He's gotten lazy with Tank gone."

Dave's expression said he agreed. "Cats are disinclined to exercise when they get older. Or maybe he just misses his old friend."

"We talked about getting a new dog, but a puppy might be too much for Grandma and Grandpa. The way things are going, we didn't want to jump into anything."

Kind. Considerate. Thoughtful.

Her parents were that and more, cornerstones of their community. And they did it together, bound by love.

"I almost wrapped up that picnic bench in time to get to the prayer service tonight," Dave noted as he leaned a hip against a strong, solid porch rail. "Hearing those bells ring, knowing what it meant, to pause and remember what we've been given, I think I did an even better job of sanding those seat boards."

"I love hearing the bells from Mountainview Church, even though it's a recording," Livvie admitted. "The area churches near my old condo had to silence their bell towers because neighbors complained."

"I can't imagine such a thing." Jane sat straighter, surprised. "Complaining about church bells? Who does that?"

"Some folks figure sleeping in is more important than going to services," Dave offered. "But I think there's something nice about getting up early and using that time to do some good."

Liv nodded, but realized she'd fallen more into the first category than the last, and that made her a little sad. Had she gotten lazy these past years? Uninvolved?

Yes.

The truth of that lay before her: her grandparents' circumstances, her lack of contact with family, keeping her distance on purpose. A sense of selfishness rose within her, but her mother put a hand on her arm, a touch that said she understood more than she let on. "It's hard to keep up with everything when we're first on our own, in a new area and newly married. Having said that, I'm mighty glad to have you here but sorry for the reasons that brought you back."

"Me, too." Her father's look said he'd be there if she wanted to talk but wouldn't pressure her. While she was grateful for that space, she knew Grandma Mason would have no such qualms.

"Grandma will not share your reserve," Livvie

reminded them. "She'll delve until she gets answers." She stood and stretched, ready for the sweet oblivion of sleep, away from failed marriages and old boyfriends. "In a way, that might be healing to both of us. Good night, guys. Love you."

They called good-night to her as she entered the house, a feeling of same-old, same-old washing over her.

She'd taken big steps backward these past few weeks. It pained her to admit it. But as she climbed the steps, the image in her head wasn't the pretty mountain painting at the ninety-degree turn, or the tiny floral wallpaper from her childhood.

It was Jack's expression as he spotted her that evening, his look, his gaze, the way his eyes sharpened in awareness.

Her gut clenched, remembering. Her heart skipped a beat.

She smacked a firm "Don't Go There" on the physical reactions. She hadn't come back here to see Jack McGuire. She'd come to regather her bearings while at a crossroads of life. To think. Plan.

Pray?

Her mother would have added that. Not Livvie. She'd prayed as a child and as a young adult, but she could see no tangible answer to prayer in her life. Sure, she had blessings in her parents, her education, and a few good friends.

But that seemed like a meager pile at age thirty.

Had prayer helped her situation with Jack eight years back?

No.

And if she was to list each instance of prayer in the past decade, she came up with a big fat zero on the response page. So be it.

But as she climbed into the old familiar bed, the memory of those bells, chiming an eventide call to worship, almost made her wish she could answer the invitation. Almost...but not quite.

"Jack, you got a minute?"

Jack turned at the top of the church steps and nodded to the new pastor of Mountainview Church of the Savior. "Ethan, yeah. What's up?"

"I heard through the grapevine—"

"Gossip mill, you mean."

Ethan Johnson's laugh said he couldn't disagree. "We'll work on that over a long, cold winter. Anyway, if you need players for the game, I'm not old-time Jasper Gulch, but I played some ball in my time. I'd be glad to fill a spot."

"Do you have a favorite position?"

"Shortstop."

Jack met the thirtysomething pastor's gaze and lowered his voice. "Folks that play now and again don't play shortstop. You good?"

"Played in a couple of district championships back in the day. Did all right." The humility in his tone didn't negate the high level of play the words *district championship* brought to Jack's mind.

"I think the Good Lord just dropped a gold mine in my lap." Jack grinned and pounded Ethan on the back. "You just filled a very important hole in our infield."

"Good."

"No college ball? You didn't go on?" Jack's baseball experience told him that most guys fielding district championship teams on the West Coast went on to play college ball or got flagged by the majors with minor-league contracts. Either way it seemed odd for Ethan to stop cold, unless his baseball career fell to an injury, like Jack's.

"Had other things to do."

Jack understood privacy. Liked it, even. In a small town known for its warp-speed information sharing, keeping things to one's self ranked high on his list. "You won't worry about offending folks from other congregations, will you? Second-guess who you're throwing out at first?"

"Not on the ball field. Which may say something's lacking about my ministerial skills, but when there's a player's mitt involved…?" Ethan hiked an eyebrow of competitive understanding. "I'm all in."

"Excellent. Thanks, Ethan. And this—" Jack glanced toward the church as Ethan locked the entry door "—was real nice tonight. Kind of peaceful and calm."

"Some days we need that, Jack. A chance to just breathe. And not think. Although your expressions tonight said you had plenty to think about."

Jack gave him a look that said yes and requested discretion, all in one.

Ethan took the hint and didn't delve. "When are we practicing?"

Jack raised his shoulders. "I have no idea. You'd think a guy who can run a cattle-and-horse ranch would have better organizational skills than this, but I never hung on the fringe of the field. I was always in the middle, working the ball, shifting angles, line of sight, so this planning stuff happened around me. How's Friday night?"

"Probably good for most, so yes. Six o'clock all right?"

Jack hadn't even thought of the practice, much less planned it, so he nodded. "Six is good."

"Want me to get the word out?"

Jack longed to jump on the idea of passing off that task to Ethan, but Rusty would have his head. Worse? He'd be right. "I'll do it. And thanks, Ethan. For both things."

"It's all right. See you Friday."

Jack logged a message into his phone to set up a Friday practice with the confirmed local players, climbed into his truck and headed home. As he passed River Road, he fought the urge to hang a left and drive to Old Trail. First, it was plain crazy to think he'd be welcome.

Second, it would be worse to start something he couldn't finish, and a woman like Olivia Franklin needed someone solid and good to stand by her.

He'd failed at baseball, then shuffled off his first career, despite the lure of big-city money. And here he was back at the ranch, which was comfortable, but nothing huge and crazy like the Shaw spread up the road.

He was the King of Mediocrity and Livvie Franklin deserved more than mediocrity in her life.

Jack heard the appreciative male whistle as he loaded barn supplies into the bed of his pickup the following morning. He turned, spotted Livvie walking down the opposite side of Main Street, realized she was the object of the whistler's attention and had to fight the urge to stalk across the road and stake his claim.

But when one of the Shaw ranch hands swung down from the back of a full-bed pickup truck and sauntered across the boardwalk to meet her, Jack crossed the road at a sharp angle, ready to interfere. He'd sort out the whys and wherefores later, but for the moment, no whistling cowboy was about to sweep Liv off her feet, so he did her a favor and intervened.

"McGuire." The cowboy didn't look all that pleased to see him. For that matter, neither did Liv. Oh, well.

"Reynolds." Jack indicated the other Shaw Ranch

cowboy with a direct gaze to the left. The second man was trying to load the truck on his own, with limited success. "Your buddy could use some help."

"I figure if he needs help, he'll let me know."

"Brent? We ain't got all day. Let's get a move on!"

Jack hid the smirk, but inside he smiled at the perfect timing. He turned back toward Liv as Brent Reynolds strode away, but Liv's cool expression said he better come up with a reason for breaking up the roadside meeting, and right quick. "I need your help."

The minute he said it, he realized it was true. He'd been lollygagging around this baseball thing, pushing himself to tackle it step by step. He realized last night his steps were too slow.

"With?" She drew the word out, her gaze on his, but her eyes stayed cool, calm and disinterested. Totally understandable, yet a kick in the teeth.

"The baseball game."

Still silent, she raised an eyebrow, one beautifully sculpted slightly-darker-than-blond brow.

"I kind of fell into this gig, and while I understand baseball one hundred and ten percent, I'm not a great organizer."

"You run a half-million-dollar beef-and-horse ranch with your father and you can't put together a local ball game?" Doubt deepened her voice. "Really, Jack?"

"Mostly really, but maybe I made that up because

I didn't want that cowboy hitting on you and I'd have grabbed any excuse in the book to walk over here and put a stop to it."

Her eyes widened. Her gaze faltered. To his dismay, a quick sheen of tears made him want to either snatch the words back or reach out and draw her into a hug he thought they both could use. "You're working on the town-history thing, right?"

She nodded, still quiet.

"Well, baseball and Jasper Gulch go hand in hand. While so many of the big towns latched on to a football mind-set, small-town baseball leagues helped settle these parts. There's almost no other place in the country that produces as many strong contenders without a public school baseball program as Jasper Gulch, Montana. And that goes straight back to the first settlers. Two of the original Shaw cousins played major-league ball, then came back and helped set up the Legion ball programs. There's a lot of bat-and-ball history here in Jasper Gulch."

The sheen of tears had disappeared. Her mixed expression said she longed to say yes but wanted to say no. He stopped talking and hoped she could move beyond the wrongs of the past....

His wrongs.

And give him a hand. Because working side by side with Livvie again would feel good and right, and not much in Jack's world felt like that of late.

"You're sure of your facts? That two of the boys played ball in the majors?"

"Twins. Chester and Lester, yes. The family called them Chet and Let. Chet played for Chicago and Let played left field for the Dodgers when they were still in New York. He actually coached Jackie Robinson for a couple of years before retiring to Florida where he worked spring training for the Dodger organization until they moved to L.A."

"There's a part of me that hates baseball, Jack."

Her words sucker punched him because of course she'd hate the game. He'd dumped her because of baseball. Correction, he'd dumped her because of his stupid, self-absorbed reaction to not being able to play. "Liv, I—"

"But—" she held up a hand to stop him, so he quieted down and listened "—I do see a direct link between the game and how things settled out here with the Shaw side of the equation. If those guys had raised families here, the makeup of the town would be entirely different. How do you know all this when you declared baseball off-limits eight years ago?"

"Coach Randolph."

The mention of the esteemed coach's name softened her expression. "I haven't seen him since I've been back. How is he, Jack?"

"He's all right. The senior league had a bunch of away games this past week, so he's been gone most nights. He lost his wife to cancer about the same time my mom died. The kind of thing that pulls folks together around here."

"Bound in grief." She thought for a few seconds before accepting. "I will help you, but on one condition."

"And that is?"

"Strictly business. No flirting, hand-holding or long, sweet looks allowed. Got it?"

"I understand. Let's shake on it."

Doubt clouded her expression as she reached out her hand, and he could tell the minute their fingers touched…clasped…that she was in over her head and knew it. He leaned down, easing the height difference between them and kept his voice soft. "Mind, Liv, I didn't say I agreed to your terms. I said I understood them. That's a whole other ball game."

"I—"

He left her sputtering as he turned to cross the street. "I'll come by tonight and we'll go over the plans, okay? Probably close to seven-thirty by the time I'm done working."

He didn't give her the opportunity to protest unless she chased him down, and he'd known Liv Franklin a long time. She wasn't the guy-chasing, make-a-scene type. But she'd be prepared to give him an earful tonight, and knowing that made him look forward to hurrying the day along.

He grabbed a bouquet of wildflowers from one of the upland meadows just before six o'clock. He could have stopped at the florist nook tucked inside the Middletons' grocery store. But if Rosemary Middleton saw him buying flowers after talking to Liv on Main Street, the entire town would be making wedding plans by sundown.

He didn't need that. Neither did Liv. But the thought of sitting side by side with her tonight, setting this baseball plan in motion…?

That notion had lightened his steps all day. When a bossy cow pushed her bovine friend into the electric-fence wire and knocked the system out, he fixed it.

When the radio offered a country tune laden with angst and dismay, he reached right over and turned it off. The ensuing silence was better than the twanging lament on life and love.

And when his father reminded him that the horse auction was coming up, his first thought went to Liv, wondering if she'd like to ride along with him to Three Forks and see what was available. The Double M was in the market for a couple of new mounts. They could grab food in town, then trailer the horses back home, together.

Shouldn't you see how tonight goes first?

He should, Jack admitted once he'd cleaned up and headed for Old Trail Road. This evening's session might be a bust. But even if it was, he had tomorrow. And the day after. And the day after that, because Liv said she was going to be in town for a while.

Which meant he'd have more time than he probably deserved, but as he steered the truck up and off the ranch property with a bouquet of yellow and purple wildflowers by his side, he figured a guy had to start making amends somewhere. This seemed as good a chance as any.

Chapter Three

Jack rethought the whole flower thing when he spotted Dave Franklin coming out of his wood shop holding a high-torque nail gun. Not that he thought Liv's father would actually shoot him full of metal brads—

He'd had plenty of opportunities these past years if that was Dave's intent.

On the other hand, Liv had been living hours away in Helena, and married.

Now things had changed and even the nicest father could be stretched too far when his daughter's husband leaves her for another woman. In any case, he left the flowers sitting on the front seat of the pickup.

"Mr. Franklin?"

"Jack."

No welcome, but no animosity, either. Jack counted that as a plus and nodded toward the house. "Liv and I are going to work together on the Old-timers' Baseball Game scheduled for the end of the month. I hope that's all right?"

"You asking permission?"

For a split second Jack thought he glimpsed a sheen of humor in the older man's eye, but when Dave faced him square, he saw nothing but calm, steady interest. "Do I need to?"

Dave sighed, glanced skyward, then drew his attention back to Jack. His face said Jack should ask permission and beg forgiveness, but his voice said something else. "No. But think hard, Jack. Real hard. You get my drift?"

He did, and couldn't disagree. "I do, sir."

"Dad? Jack?" Livvie stepped onto the porch, and when she did, the melon-rinsed tones of the westward arching sun faded, she was that pretty. "You giving him the third degree, Dad?"

"The temptation's mighty strong, Liv."

"But?" She met her father's gaze with a look that coached his next reply.

"You're old enough to take care of yourself and are inclined to do just that."

Liv smiled as she came down the stairs, slipped an arm around her father's waist and hugged him. "Well said."

"Since you told me what to say, that's no surprise. I've lived with your mother for nearly forty years. If nothing else, I've learned how to follow directions." Humor marked Dave's face for real this time.

It was clear he enjoyed having Livvie back home, but equally clear he didn't want her hurt again.

Neither did Jack, and the thought of flirting with a woman who might still love her ex-husband—a conniving cheat who didn't deserve an amazing woman like Olivia Franklin in the first place—helped keep things in perspective. "I brought some notes you might be able to use for the history thing."

Liv took the sheaf of paper from Jack's hand. For just a moment their fingers grazed, barely a touch, but enough to make Jack long to take her hand in his. Hold it snug and chat about things that would keep her smile firmly in place.

That's what had been missing last night, he realized. Liv's smile, broad and sweet. Inviting. Her contagious laugh, the kind that made heads turn and folks join in for no particular reason.

Her smile today said she was doing all right, but a woman like Liv should never be doing just all right. She should be happy, joyous and cheerful. The way she used to be, he remembered.

As he followed her up to the porch, he wondered if that girl still existed, or if the men in her life had ruined something as precious and sweet as a young woman's joy.

Shame knifed him, but as Liv settled into the corner of the porch glider, another realization hit. God had given him this chance to make things right. But maybe he could do more than simply mend old wrongs. Maybe he could restore Liv's joyful spirit, the smiling peace that used to reign within her.

He sank into the rocker and watched as she perused the papers. "Jack…" She paused and sat forward with a start, and for a brief moment he read the excitement of old in her eyes. She pointed to an item on the paper he'd printed off the internet. "This says that Lester helped bury the time capsule."

"That's important?"

Liv inched closer to show him the printed lines referring to Lester Shaw and nodded. "It could be. With the capsule missing, and no one knowing what was in it, what went on, or why anyone would steal an old memory box from a hundred years ago, maybe someone in Lester's branch of the family knows something. Maybe he told his family what was in the box. Knowing what was in there might help deputy Cal Calloway and the sheriff's office figure out why it was taken. There could be some tidbit of information that will clear up this whole mess." She ticked off two fingers as she continued, "The missing capsule. The fire at the rodeo. Things like this might seem minor in big cities, but in Jasper Gulch…? A tucked-in-a-nook town with generations of the same families living here decade by decade?" Her look of remorse underscored her meaning. "Criminal stuff like that could pull a small town like ours apart."

It made sense, but… "Lester never married. Chet

did, it's in his baseball records, but Lester died a bachelor. Does it say anything about Chet being involved with the capsule burial?"

She shook her head. The scent of spiced vanilla grabbed him by the throat and wouldn't let go. The smell drew him closer, ostensibly to look at the history papers she held out, but what he really wanted was one more breath of that sweet country smell, gently spiced.

Liv's scent.

"Well."

She seemed totally uninspired by his new proximity, so he leaned back in his chair, reclaiming a proper distance in case Dave came around with that nail gun again.

"I'm going to keep these, if that's okay?" She looked up and he nodded, pretending he didn't want to draw closer because they both knew better. Well, she knew better, and he'd just promised her father to think hard and long before starting something he couldn't finish. Not as if he was even considering starting something with a woman on the rebound, because that rarely boded well. "It's fine."

"And can I look at what you've got lined up for the game so far?"

Sheepish, he handed over the half-filled single sheet of paper. She stared at the single sheet as if appalled, then made a show of unfolding it—

Examining the empty back side while a mix of dismay and bemusement darkened her features—

Refolding it and looking at him, expectant. "That's it? To field two teams? The Bombers and the Bobcats?"

"Well, the new pastor's going to play shortstop for us, and he's good, so we've got one more player. And a few I haven't heard back from. So we've almost got one team manned."

"Did you give them a follow-up call?"

He hadn't, no. He swallowed hard and admitted, "I texted them."

The look on her face said he was clueless, and he couldn't argue the fact. He hated phones, barely liked people and only took this on because guilt over Wes's condition pushed him to say yes.

"First, this game is a big deal for the town, right?"

"Yes."

"Second, not everyone is comfortable texting, and some of these guys are in their sixties and seventies, Jack. They might not even have texting capabilities in their phones."

She was right, of course.

"And third, for something special like this, do you think the New York Yankees send out a text to their former players about their annual Old-timers' Day? No, they call and invite them to play. It's an honor to be asked and an honor to be called."

A hint of light began shining at the end of his self-imposed tunnel vision. "So, would you—"

"I would not." She didn't even let him get the

words out of his mouth before refusing, and that said the woman before him was tougher than the girl she'd been a decade before. "But I will help organize the concessions, the flyers and the contact lists for endorsements and sponsors to raise money for the new museum. This way we're both benefiting from our combined efforts."

"You're benefiting because it's raising money for something you love," Jack objected. He clapped a hand to the base of his neck and scowled. "I fail to see the benefit to me in all this."

"It gets you out of the saddle, off the ranch and into the mainstream of life again, which is where we all should be. You can thank me later." She went inside and came back with a landline phone and a small laptop computer. She handed the phone to him and he had no option but to take it. "Use this. The cell coverage is spotty out here, but you can get hold of most of the guys while I'm working on a sketch and a list for concessions."

He had no choice.

She knew it, he could tell from the way she tipped her chin and offered the phone as if passing a baseball to a new pitcher on the mound.

He hated making phone calls and didn't like seeking favors, but the way Liv phrased it, as if asking folks to take part in the centennial was a privilege, made it easier to dial that first number. And when the old right fielder who now lived in northern Idaho gave him an enthusiastic yes and thanked him for the invite, Jack sat back. "He's coming. Excited, even. And he thanked me for calling."

She glanced up from her note-making and her gaze didn't say "I told you so." It said his words made her happy, that taking charge and doing what he needed to do made her proud.

A little thing, making a few phone calls. By the time he was done, he had eight more firm yesses, two I'm-sorry-can't-make-its and had left three messages to voice mail. So far so good. And it felt good, too, which made his dread of doing it fairly ridiculous.

"Did you call Pete Daniels?" Liv looked up from her email account as she invited area nonprofits and business owners to take part in the game-day festivities. "I heard he was good."

Jack set the phone down, frowned and shook his head. "No."

"You've got a solid player right here in town and you're dissing him? Why?"

"Several reasons."

Liv's quiet posture invited him to continue.

"Pete's a hothead. He sets players off. He annoys the umpires. He's got a chip on his shoulder and he's rude. He's got great playing skills but is that the kind of attitude we want representing the town at the big game?"

"No," Liv agreed. "I knew he'd played for a bunch of years. Dad sent me the town paper from time to time, and I saw Pete's stats now and again.

But you're right, there's no reason to intentionally bring in someone whose attitude can mess up a fun game like this. You've got the rest of the guys contacted, though?"

"I do."

He'd done it in less than an hour and from the wealth of notes Liv had on her laptop, it looked as if they had wrapped up a good deal of the planning in one short evening.

Which meant they could pretty much be all done, but that was the last thing he wanted to be, so he plunged in, wanting at least one more day of working side by side with Livvie Franklin. "Liv, we've done well tonight, but shouldn't we get together again to firm things up? I've got a rancher from Wyoming coming in to look at calves tomorrow night, but I'm free the night after."

She scanned her notes, then him, with no discernible change of expression. "Aren't we just about done? I'll get hold of the ladies' auxiliary and the Jasper Gulch Hose Company about doing the food. The firefighters do the best chicken barbecue, and that way they can make money for their organizations, while the take at the gate goes to the museum. I'm sure the Sports Boosters will man their hot dog and hamburger stand like they do for the Legion games. If the high school band can do the national anthem and we get someone to sing "Take Me Out to the Ball Game" at the seventh-inning stretch, we're set, right?"

Jack thought hard and quick. "But what about the flyers? Posting them and getting them done? And by the way, I'm heading to Three Forks on Saturday for the horse auction, and I was wondering if you'd like to tag along."

She sat back. Stared at him. In fact, she stared at him so long that he half wondered if she'd gone into some kind of shock, but before he could dial 911, her mother's voice chimed in from the garden around the corner. "Liv, that would be fun, don't you think? Dad and I are leaving on Saturday and you were just saying how you wanted a chance to reacquaint yourself with riding while you were here."

"You said that?" Jack leaned forward. Her mother's reminder had chased the deer-in-the-headlights look from Liv's eyes, but her current expression said her mother would most likely get an earful when Jack was gone. "So, come, then. We'll grab food up there. We'd have to take off around eight in the morning. That all right with you?"

She longed to refuse his offer.

She wanted to hurl his stupid invite back at him and remind him of how many nights she'd spent crying in her pillow. Did he have any clue the amount of money she'd wasted on lotion-treated tissues?

But the other part of her, the part that had gotten downright excited when she passed the Jasper

Gulch, Montana, Welcomes You! sign, knowing she'd see Jack again—*the more traitorous side*—said, "Yes. I'll be ready at eight. Should I bring anything along?"

Jack stood and shook his head. "Naw, if you email me a copy of your notes and plans, we'll be good. I'll print them up at home. And Livvie?" He turned as he got to the stairs, looking for all the world as if he wanted to stay, but the cool expression she aimed his way said there was no reason to linger. "Thanks so much for this." He held up the paper that now held eighteen players. "I couldn't have done it without you."

"You could have but were choosing not to," she corrected him smoothly. "And that's not the Jack I knew. That Jack took everything in stride, the good, the bad and the ugly, and went with it. Until you hurt your arm."

She refused to sugarcoat his actions. He'd let an injury change him, alter his ways, upset his life. He faced her, looking uncertain, but then dipped his chin in acknowledgment. "It was a stupid thing to do, Liv, and I'm sorry."

She studied him for long seconds, squinted slightly, then nodded. "It's a start."

A start. That's what he'd wanted, right? A new beginning, a chance to mend old wrongs, set things right. She got up and walked him to the truck, and when he opened the door, the scent of wildflowers escaped in a rush of late-summer sweetness. Liv sniffed the air and spotted the bouquet. Realization brightened her face as she tipped her head back to look up at him. "You brought me flowers."

"Yes. And then chickened out when your father approached with his nail gun."

A tiny grin lit her face like a morning sunrise. "So. What now?"

He frowned, not understanding.

She directed her look to the flowers. "Do I get them now?"

"I— Um…they're kind of sad looking now, aren't they?"

She shook her head as he reached across the seat to grasp the slightly wilted bouquet. "A good drink of water and they'll spruce up fine."

"You think?"

"Yup." She reached out and he set the somewhat woebegone flowers in her hand. "Water's an amazing thing."

"'With joy you shall draw water,'" Jack began, and when Liv finished the sweet words of Isaiah, his heart opened just a little bit more.

"'From the streams of salvation.'"

"You remembered."

"Your mother has that painted on the little sign above your barn doors. Is it still there?"

It was, kind of like most everything else his mother had done or placed. He and Dad hadn't moved much of anything. At first that was fine.

Now it seemed like neither one knew how to start the process of change. "It is. I think of her every time I walk into that section of the barn."

"She was a wonderful person, Jack. And she wanted you to be happy."

He frowned, glanced down and shrugged. "I kind of blew that, didn't I?"

"Then? Yes. Now?" She gazed up at him once more, and the look she offered him said he wasn't doing all that badly and that made him feel good inside. Really good. "I think you are happy now. Happy to be here, to be part of the ranch, the town. As long as you break the hermit habit, I expect you'll do just fine, Jack McGuire."

Funny how words could make things seem real. Hearing her assessment, he felt better. As if he was taking big leaps instead of small steps. Was that because he was moving with more force or because Livvie showed faith in him?

Maybe both. He smiled down at her and raised his hand, gently grazing her left cheek with one work-roughened finger. "Thanks, Liv. For everything."

"And thank you." She stepped back, creating a distance, but raised the bouquet slightly. "I love the flowers."

He climbed into the truck feeling better than he had in a long while, and as he backed down the driveway, the sight of her standing there, holding a bouquet of native-grown flowers in her hand, made him wonder what she'd look like as a bride.

Would she consider getting married again? Ever?

Would she consider you trustworthy enough to take a chance on, you mean? Probably not. You broke her heart once. Why would she trust you to treasure it again?

Because he was older. More mature. Stronger. More faithful.

Actions speak louder than words, his conscience reminded him, and it sounded slightly doubtful. *Give it your best shot, but you heard her father. Think hard. Real hard.*

He would, Jack decided. But he wouldn't just think hard this time. He'd pray. Something as important as Liv's happiness deserved God on their side.

He'd been a churchgoer for a long time. But the past few years he'd felt as if he was just going through the motions. As if maybe he didn't really belong.

He'd wondered if others felt like that, but it wasn't something he talked about. But the other night, when Ethan talked about redeeming love and God's sacrificial nature, the young pastor's words hit home.

Jack wanted redeeming love. He didn't know if he could fix things with Livvie, but he knew that just making things better would benefit both of them. Heal them. And Jesus was a healer, so the mathematics of the situation should work.

Redeeming love, simple yet powerful. He longed for that. Needed it. And he wanted to be the kind of gentle, loving person that deserved it. Starting now.

"Nice flowers, honey."

Liv heard the amusement in her mother's voice and faced her as she gave the arrangement a much-needed drink. "Thanks. They've been through a troubling experience tonight, but I think they'll perk up by morning."

"There's an analogy for you."

"Me and the flowers?" Liv made a face but couldn't refute her mother's logic. "True enough. What time are you guys pulling out on Saturday?"

"Around five. I'll try not to wake you."

"Well, I told Jack I'd ride to Three Forks for the horse auction, so I'll be up early anyway. Thanks for the obvious nudge, by the way."

"You're welcome." Her mother shrugged and grinned. "You're helping him with the game—"

"And he's giving me info about the old-time baseball history of Jasper Gulch," Liv inserted. "All business, Mom."

"Mmm-hmm." Jane flicked the flowers a glance. "A private evening planning session, flowers and a date. Is that the way business is done these days, dear?"

"Small-town business, yes. If we met in town,

every tongue would be wagging. Half the town has us married already, because how on earth can two single people not end up together when fate and time thrust them into the same hometown?"

"Memories go back a ways. And folks liked seeing you as a couple. But you're right, that was a long time ago and a lot has changed. And you tried a long-distance relationship with Jack once and it didn't work. If you get a job in one of the cities, that would be rough on both of you. Of course, you could stay here," her mother added as she hugged Liv good-night. "I won't deny that I love having you home. But I also know that jobs are scarce and you need to make a living, so I won't pester you about it."

"Any more than you already have." Liv lifted the vase and turned to carry it up the stairs. "Me and my flowers are going to bed. I'm going to practice getting up early the next couple of days so I don't mess up Saturday morning. It would be just like me to hit the snooze alarm and wake up to Jack pounding on the door, ready to hit the trail."

Jane's expression said she approved of the practice mornings. While she'd said nothing the past week, Liv had noted the concern on her mother's face the longer Liv stayed in bed each day. Seeing that worry made her want more jump in her step, but coming back to Jasper Gulch held up a dulled mirror image. No job, no marriage, no family.

In baseball talk, three strikes was an out. But seeing Jack after all this time? Working with him?

That made her feel as if she was back at home plate, bat in hand, a new opportunity waiting. Silly, yes. But it didn't feel silly, it felt real and good and wholesome.

One bouquet of wildflowers and you're jumping into the batter's box again? Have you learned nothing from your past experiences?

Liv cringed as she set the flowers onto a small plate, protecting the oil finish on the antique dresser. Maybe she should exercise more caution.

Maybe?

She hauled in a deep breath. She would use more caution and maintain a distance from Jack. Too much too soon, and she had no desire to make herself the talk of the town or mess up her life again. Therefore, she resolved to keep things to "friends only" status with Jack McGuire. She'd been taught a tough lesson by her baseball-loving ex-boyfriend years back. It was time for her to smarten up. Read the pitches. An easy walk to first base was way better than adding to her current strike list. She'd put Jack into the "Danger Zone" as she drove into town… Now she needed to keep him there.

Sitting an hour in the front seat of his pickup, back and forth to Three Forks?

She made a face into the mirror, because she was having trouble keeping her distance with wide-open space around them. How much trickier would it be in close proximity?

A part of her toyed with the idea of texting Jack to back out.

The other part?

She studied the face in the mirror and faced facts. The other part was wishing time away, anxious to see Jack again. The rueful expression looking back at her said she was in trouble…big trouble… Knowing that trouble concerned Jack McGuire made her heart beat faster, and that was a feeling she'd been missing for a long time.

Chapter Four

The cheerful whistling trill caught Jack off guard on Friday morning. He straightened as the sound approached the barn, then realized he'd been hearing it in the background for a while, an old sound, normal and nice.

Except it hadn't been normal since his mother passed away, which made the sound of his father's easy tune an even better surprise. He turned as Mick strode through the wide doors at the far end. The older McGuire spotted Jack and moved his way. "That part came in." He held out an oblong box, open along one side.

"Good." Jack set the box aside and nodded west. "I should have enough time to get those hydraulics working again before the rain comes. Then we can bring that hay alongside."

"Need help?"

"I don't, but I appreciate the offer. And you don't

look like you're dressed for dirt diving beneath a John Deere in any case."

"I said I'd help tear off some bad porch planking for a friend," his father explained, but the way he said it, as if helping a friend was slightly uncomfortable, surprised Jack. Mick McGuire might be a quiet guy, but he was always willing to help whoever needed an extra hand. Although he looked mighty nice to be leveraging old wood and rusty nails. "Figured with rain coming, today was as good as any."

"Ripping up boards?" Jack cast his father's clean shirt and jeans a doubtful look. "You got cleaned up to get dirty?"

His father shrugged, but the look on his face, as if he'd just been caught with a hand in the cookie jar, made Jack think hard and quick. His father wasn't just going to help a friend.

He was going to help a *woman* friend.

That explained the cologne and the clean-shaven face.

"Call if you need me." Mick gave a short wave and aimed for the truck.

"Right." Reality made Jack straighten and watch his father leave. "See ya'."

Mick strolled out of the barn, his gait easy, the roll of his shoulders a dead giveaway. He settled a couple of toolboxes into the bed of his signature red Double M pickup truck. Then he climbed into the driver's seat with the window open, the radio cranking Easton Corbin sounding like a young George Strait. As the truck rounded the curved driveway, Jack saw his father's head bob in time with the music…and heard him start to whistle along as the truck headed for the road.

His father. Cleaned up, whistling and headed out for the day.

The irony of how he planned to do the same thing the following morning wasn't lost on Jack. He'd huffed about all the centennial nonsense. He'd done his best to ignore it until the rodeo rumbled into town last month and Julie Shaw cornered him.

But maybe Jasper Gulch needed something new to shake things up. A town mired in the past, arguing over moving forward, tussling about fixing a long-broken bridge. A place with little crime, beset with strange stuff lately. The time capsule disappearance. Problems at the rodeo. The shed there being set on fire. Troubling things in a town that boasted no crime other than errant dogs and cows now and again traipsing over flower beds they didn't own.

On the plus side, Liv had come back, at least for a little while. Shop owners had spruced up their storefronts on Main Street and the access roads. Bright banners welcomed folks to town and the whole thing looked more inviting than normal.

The changing light reminded him of the storm front headed their way, but the nice thing about hauling fresh-rolled hay up to the barnyard was that he had plenty of time to think. And since seeing Livvie earlier in the week, he didn't mind thinking nearly as much as he used to.

Blue jeans and a shirt. What could be difficult about that?

Everything.

And her hair. Ponytail? Down?

Ponytail, Liv decided as she bent over, smoothed the front with the brush and gathered her hair into a band.

She frowned in the mirror, added a lace cami, then refastened the jeweled snaps on the short-sleeved fitted shirt and nodded at the new image.

Cowgirl, with emphasis on "girl." She grabbed her Stetson and had her boots on before Jack pulled up to the curb with the four-horse trailer attached. Jack strolled to the porch as she stepped outside, and the look on his face said he'd been looking forward to this morning, just like her. Which meant she'd be the one to put the brakes on. "Hey, cowboy."

"Hey, yourself." He gave the brim of his hat the slightest of tweaks and watched her smile. "You still remember how it's done."

"You can take the girl out of the country, but you can't take the country out of the girl."

"And who'd want to?" Jack's expression said that was about the stupidest thing he'd ever heard. The look on his face made Liv revisit her years away.

Her expression must have changed, because Jack leaned forward and ducked a little to see her face. "Didn't mean to insult. And in the city, they wear what they want, but if the look suits, and in your case, I think you were born to ride and wear Western—"

His compliment made her smile because she did feel at home in these clothes. Natural. And maybe younger than she'd felt the last few years.

"Why not embrace it at least as long as you're here?" He held the truck door open and Liv couldn't remember the last time Billy had held the door open for her. If ever. She pushed the comparison aside as Jack climbed into the driver's seat. He shoved the truck into gear and headed for Route 287. He made the turn onto the two-lane and pushed his hat back. "So here's my plan." He indicated her notebook and iPad. "We can talk baseball and history all you want. I invited Coach over tomorrow, so I was hoping you could come by the ranch for supper and we can pick Coach's brain, too."

"Except he didn't live around here until twenty years ago and has no family here," Liv pointed out. "I'd love to see him, but can't we get together in town?"

"On a Sunday evening?" Jack's look said she needed to remember where she was, and he was right. Jasper Gulch embraced limited business hours on Sunday, something she hadn't seen much in the city. Out of respect for family time and the Lord's Day, nothing was open in Jasper Gulch on Sunday evenings. "Besides, I owe Coach a dinner, and we might as well grill a few steaks and throw some potatoes in the fire, don't you think? No biggie."

It was a biggie, and he knew it. She read him like an open book on a sunlit afternoon, but she'd be lying if she said she didn't want to have supper at the ranch, and she'd made a promise to herself on the way back to Jasper Gulch nearly two weeks before. No more pretense. Face life, get a grip and be honest with herself. So she squared her shoulders and nodded as she began making notes. "It does sound good, and with Mom and Dad away I'm not prone to cooking for one, so you've saved me from starvation."

"Good."

She ignored the quick grin he cast her way as she waited for her screen to refresh. "And that way I can check on how our new friends are doing. If we find any today, that is. How's Dillinger?" Dillinger had been her horse of choice at the Double M through the years they dated. Jack would mount Roy-O, the large bay, and she'd saddle Dillinger, the strong-willed buckskin that reminded her of Denny in *The Man from Snowy River*. A good horse, brave and true.

Jack sucked in a breath. His hesitation said more than words.

"He's gone?"

"Back in February. Winters are hard on old animals."

"Like Tank." She breathed deep and stared out the window, the rise of mountains curving this way and that, rugged land stretching in every direction. "I forgot that being away for so many years really changes things. People gone. Animals gone. Except for the beginnings of the new museum, the town has stayed the same on the surface." She bit back a sigh from somewhere deep inside as reality bit deep. "But the real things? The important ones, like losing people and things you love? I'm realizing how much I've missed by being gone."

"Time goes on." Jack paused at a fork in the road, bore right and then added, "And just the idea of that museum caused a ruckus with folks."

"Why?" She turned to face him and had to steel herself not to get lost in his profile. Seeing him… hearing him…simple proximity *to* him brought back all kinds of memories. She'd held hard to the last memories, her broken heart, weeks of tears, years of living in the same Midwestern city while avoiding him at all costs, but now? Here in Jasper Gulch? The good memories were starting to edge out the bad ones, and she couldn't let that happen.

"Jackson Shaw likes things the way they are. Always has, always will. His son Adam and the other kids are more easygoing, and Cord's actually been fighting his father on the whole bridge issue—"

"Cord wants the bridge fixed?" Livvie sat back, surprised. "Good for him. Just because Jackson is the mayor doesn't make him the law."

Jack shot her a look that said "get real" and Liv sighed. "Okay, I get it. But just because it *is* that way doesn't mean it should be. Three cheers for Cord standing up on his own. And I heard Julie's raising sheep on a farm section, so clearly Jackson's kids are trying to find their own paths."

"Nadine's influence on top of Jackson's stubbornness."

"Mothers can be a formidable force, even the gentle ones." Liv laughed, thinking of her mother's strength and wisdom. "Good for Nadine."

A sign for Three Forks came into view as Jack rounded a curve. He eased up on the gas. "I was thinking we could get ribs at Willow Creek for dinner."

The place with melt-in-your-mouth ribs that she and Jack had loved when they spent college breaks in Jasper Gulch? A place they enjoyed thoroughly until the breakup that rivaled the big bang with hometown repercussions? Um, no. Not about to happen. "A sandwich is fine. We don't need to go to any trouble or try to be fancy."

"I've never heard ribs called fancy." Jack's voice stayed easy, but Liv knew he was calling her out.

"Let's keep it simple, Jack. You. Me. The horses. And a sandwich."

"You're warning me off."

Yes and no. "I'm protecting both of us from repeating the mistakes of the past," she explained. She kept her voice even, but it was crazy difficult to manage with Jack sitting inches away. But she did it because self-protection was a hard lesson learned. "You've got your life. I've got mine. For the moment our paths have intersected while we both work on a mutually beneficial project. Let's keep it at that."

He sent her a look that stammered her heart, and delivered a cockeyed smile, to boot. "A sandwich it is, then. Although if we happen to be downwind of Willow Creek's smoker and you change your mind, I got us midafternoon reservations, and they weren't easy to come by, either."

"But the horses…?"

"Bo Gravinger's on hand. He said he'll mind things for us to get a bite. But a sandwich is fine, too, Liv. It's not the food near as much as the nice company. That's a pleasure right there."

Her off-rhythm heart swelled at his words. The tone of voice, the tilt of his chin, the easy smile that worked his jaw just so.

Her resolve went south in a hurry because she'd like nothing better than to spend long hours relaxing with Jack, eyeing horses, sharing food on a bright summer's day. He pointed to the left as he eased the truck and trailer into a parking area off to the right. "Nice crowd and good potential. Let's go find us some horses, little lady."

Adorable, handsome and available.

She'd vowed to steel her heart and emotions against all three. The reality of trying to do that while checking out beautiful mounts for the Double M rancher and his dad?

Virtually impossible.

"The two-year-old dark bay stallion." Liv kept her voice low as they surveyed the groups of horses surrounding the near paddock. Jack eyed the solid young potential stud and agreed.

"I was thinking exactly the same." The fact that they both selected the same young horse with breeding potential wasn't lost on Jack. They'd always been on the same page, back in the day. But that was years ago, and a pile of mistakes since to work through. "Good temperament, great look, and stands solid."

"Stunning look, actually," Liv corrected him. "Not too proud, ready for direction, anxious to please. If those qualities pass down to offspring, you've got a gold-mine stallion right there. And the contrast of the black mane and tail sweeten the effect."

"Anyone else strike you today?"

She slanted her gaze up to him with an expression that said yes, something else did strike her, but it was off-limits and out of reach. Then she settled her shoulders, climbed the rail and waved to the outer edge. "You've got matching bay fillies over there, a pretty pair and not a bit flighty. Wanna walk around and check them out?"

"It's a four-horse trailer, so sure. Let's go." He reached out and grasped her waist to swing her down, but when her feet touched the dusty ground, the last thing he wanted to do was let go. In fact—

"This way, cowboy. And keep your mind on the horses."

"Yes, ma'am." He grinned behind her, properly chastised but knowing she only half meant it. As they rounded the far end of the west-facing corral, the pair of fillies danced left, then settled as Liv moved closer, crooning. Another interested buyer shot them a look and gave up his spot near the fence, and when Jack asked the owner to bring the ladies by, he watched as Liv examined each one. "What's the verdict?"

She faced him. "Sound. Fine. Pretty. Calm for their age."

"Their lineage has breed-stock potential written all over it."

"Is that a problem?"

Jack ran a hand across the nape of his neck, thoughtful. "Time is shorter without Mom. And the ranch hands are good guys, but it takes a special touch to work with broodmares."

Liv had that touch, the crucial elemental mix

of gentle but firm direction, the soft voice horses preferred. She'd helped his mother with the mares often as a teen. But she wasn't staying, and how awkward would it be to offer her a job on the ranch? She'd laugh him out of the paddock.

"I can help while I'm here."

Jack paused. Turned. When his eyes locked with hers, the solid ball that had been his heart for too many years began to soften, making it easy and hard to breathe all at once. "You wouldn't mind?"

She looked off over his right shoulder, then drew her attention back his way. The filly nickered and nosed Liv, as if pushing her to say yes. The horse's action made Liv smile and she looped an arm around the filly's neck. "Do I get naming rights if I sign on?"

Naming rights and more, but Jack had worked with skittish animals all his life, and while Liv wasn't an anxious foal, she had plenty of reason to doubt his good intentions, so he'd go slow and easy. "Yup."

"Deal."

"Sweet." He bumped knuckles with her as the bullhorn called folks to the sale arena. "Let's go in. Want coffee?"

"No. I'll wait until we eat later. But thank you."

"My pleasure." And it was, he realized. As he followed her into the crowded ringside seats, he developed a hearty appreciation for her well-fitted jeans and sassy boots. Her tan Stetson, the same hat she'd worn years ago, still bore a tiny grease stain from a barbecue they'd attended together as college sophomores, a great night of planning for the future. A future he'd thrown away in a fit of anger. How stupid and childish that seemed now.

Yes, he loved baseball. The game, the sport, the teamwork. But he should have been more mature and accepting. Wasn't that what Ethan had talked about last Monday? Accepting what is and making the best of your situation to help others?

He'd done nothing like that eight years ago. In truth, he'd done nothing like that since, either, other than helping his mother through her illness, but a thin surge of energy seemed to be building inside him, making him think he could do anything again.

"These seats okay?" Liv turned about halfway up the steps, and her look of amusement said she'd caught him out. "Business, Jack. Not monkey business."

He laughed, settled into the seat next to her, leaned back and folded his arms behind his head. "Just thinking how fun it will be to have you back on the ranch, helping with things. It's been too long, Livvie. Way too long."

Too long?

His words spiked her pulse and his gaze said he'd take things slow, but sitting there with him, sorting horseflesh for the future of the Double M, the familiar sounds and scents of the stockyard drew her in. She couldn't imagine being anywhere else. And yet she would be somewhere else soon. Her position in Helena had folded and they'd given her a decent severance package, but she'd need a job and a place to live before too long.

The auctioneer keyed his mike and began welcoming the crowd of buyers and sellers as Liv considered her choices. For the moment, helping Jack, working on the town history and hanging with horses was enough. More than enough. She'd face the job market Monday morning, searching out possibilities on the internet, but that left her Saturday and Sunday to enjoy ranch work, a nice respite from years of city living and an eight-by-eight windowless cubicle. And when Jack successfully outbid other potential buyers for the matched bay fillies and the gorgeous red stallion, she accompanied him around back to finish the deal, heady with the thought of gathering the horses and heading home.

"Randy, hey." Jack stuck out a hand to the rancher from northern Idaho and nodded to the pair. "They're beauties. Tell your mother they'll be in good hands."

"Tell her yourself, she's right over there." Randy Malcolm pointed beyond Liv. "She rode along to grab a rescue on the way up. He's in sorry shape, but she heard about him on Facebook and decided he needed a new start."

"Jack. Look." Liv pointed to the horse facing them from the back of the Malcolm trailer. "It's—"

"He looks like Dillinger." Jack stared hard at the faded, neglected image of his former beloved buckskin, Liv's favorite mount on the ranch.

"He does. Can we—?" She stared up at him, imploring, trying to read the look on his face. He scrubbed a hand to the back of his neck and faced her direct. "You're willing to come work with him? Cater to him? He'll need lots of time and care, sun and rest, and we're in August already."

"Yes."

"You didn't sound so sure inside."

"Well, I am now." She set her jaw and folded her arms. "Go see Mrs. Malcolm and ask if she'll let us take him."

"We'll go see her." He put the emphasis on the plural pronoun. "I can't jump into this alone, and if we mess that horse up Joy Malcolm will drive down from Idaho with a switch to tan my hide. I like my hide just the way it is, thank you. So think hard before we head over there."

"I don't have to think hard, I've made my decision."

"Well, then." An easy smile spread across Jack's face, a look that said he'd just won a battle. He extended a hand her way, a gesture that meant she was on board for all that helping the horse entailed. "Welcome back to the Double M, little lady."

She accepted his hand, shook once, hard and

firm, but then didn't squawk when he wrapped his left hand around her right as they crossed the dusty lot to see Joy Malcolm about a beat-up horse who needed tender loving care. Her hand felt right and good, melded with his, and she'd worry about the whys and wherefores later. Because right now, surrounded by horses, cowboys, trucks, trailers and hot August dust, she felt at peace.

"If we do this," Jack said, nodding toward the horse tucked in the left fore side of the Malcolms' travel rig, "we'll probably have to eat on the run. We'll want to get this guy home and tended without stopping."

"Front-seat burgers work for me." She didn't hesitate as they approached Joy's rig, she simply let go of Jack's hand and moved forward, ready to deal. "Mrs. Malcolm, your rescue looks a lot like a horse I loved back in the day. Jack and I—" she indicated Jack with a quick look his way "—would like to take him in, if at all possible. I'm sure you—"

"Darlin', if you're tellin' me that you and Jack can take this sorry animal and give him a good home on the Double M, save your breath. I'm sold. I just couldn't sit back and ignore him, and I knew Randy was coming to auction. But I've got two grandchildren and six foals on the way, plus cattle to ride herd on. I'm busy enough and maybe this was just one of those things that was meant to be."

"You're sure?" Pleasure rose up within Liv. "You don't mind us stepping in?"

"Not a bit, and we can load him right now with the fillies you bought. I was tempted to keep them, such a nice pair, but Randy's father reminded me that babies take time and with two daughters due, I needed to pick my battles this year."

"Thank you!" Liv reached out and hugged the older woman impulsively, wanting to say so much more, but that would probably seem ridiculous to a staunch ranch wife like Joy Malcolm.

The older woman surprised her by putting a hand on each side of Liv's face, then smiling down at her. "Years ago I found myself by working with a horse like this." She shrugged one shoulder toward the faded gelding. "It gave me time to think, time to pray and time to court Randy's father." She smiled and released Liv's cheeks with a little pat to her shoulders. "I am often amazed by how God manages to plunk us right in the middle of where we're supposed to be when we least expect it, so yes. You take this horse and love on him all you can before the weather turns sharp. Nothing like healing together, young lady."

Her words stirred something else inside Livvie, a truth she'd been unwilling to admit.

She needed healing. She needed peace. She needed to look in the mirror and not see a loser who'd had two men run out on her. The fact that her ex-husband had already remarried his extramarital girlfriend bit deep into her bruised ego. Tossing a baby into the mix meant Billy hadn't wasted any time and was perfectly willing to start a family with someone.

Just not her.

The horse nickered softly as Joy guided him out of the trailer. His mild voice said, "What now?" but as Liv ran a gentle hand down his neck, she whispered into his ear, "Now we go home, my friend. Now we go home."

She took the lead and walked the horse across the lot. Animal movement had stirred the dust. Particulated Montana topsoil hazed the midday air.

Liv didn't care. She walked the gelding into the trailer, placing him between the mares. If the young stallion they loaded from the other side thought to kick up a fuss, she wanted two steady, well-fed horses to let him know they weren't impressed. This malnourished fellow shouldn't be put to the test today. Not until he had a few weeks of TLC and food.

"We're all set?" Jack asked as she settled the horse and closed the ramp.

"Good to go. Thanks for loading the girls, Randy."

"My pleasure. And right back at ya' for taking him off Mom's hands. While we didn't need extra work, I couldn't see letting him be put down. I'm grateful."

"No." Jack faced him, and stuck out a hand. "We are. Travel with care."

"Will do. You, too." They shook hands as Liv

climbed into the front seat of the big truck. She waved to the dashboard clock as she withdrew her phone. "There's a great burger joint about fifteen minutes out. I'm going to call and order food so we don't have to keep these guys waiting. I'm grabbing a mushroom Swiss burger and fries. How about you?"

"Sounds perfect. Ask them to put ketchup, pickles and sweet relish on mine."

"Done." She found the number online, called in the order and settled into her seat after scanning the trailer a quick look. "What a day."

"Great. Wonderful. There are now four horses ready to call the Double M home. Including your new project."

She heard the emphasis on the pronoun, but wasn't about to disagree. Her heart had seized upon first seeing the horse and hadn't let go yet. Maybe it was learning of Dillinger's demise. Maybe it was searching for times lost but never forgotten. Or maybe she empathized with the horse, wanting them both healed and loved. That thought touched a nerve, but she scuttled it and kept her voice bright with anticipation. "I can't wait to get him home, get him cleaned up. Feed him. Brush him. Talk to him."

"You've got a knack, for sure. Always did have. The thing is…" His voice trailed off and he looked uncertain.

"The thing is?"

"Are you wasting all those years of education

being back here? There's not much in the way of work for someone with all those degrees, and you're so smart, Livvie. Always were." Trouble tinged his tone, as if second-guessing way more than trailering a group of horses home to a Montana ranch. "Will you feel like you're wasting all that time and money to help with a crowd of horses the next few months?"

His words made her pause, but then she shrugged. "I might have thought so the last few years because I was caught up in my job. I poured myself into research work and did well with it, but if I look back truthfully…" She drew a breath and turned to see him more directly. "If you asked me then if I was happy, I'd have said yes. I thought I was flying high, doing well. But looking back, I see it different and that's because I'm facing the truth about my life then. Clearly that's easier at a distance."

Jack's grimace said he agreed.

"It will be a little crazy living at home, especially if Grandma and Grandpa move in, but you know what, Jack?" She smiled when he spiked his right brow to show he was listening. "I think I can be a help to them and my parents. I'm beginning to see there's more to life than hefty paychecks and bylines in university presses and museum trade magazines. I forgot how nice this all is." She waved a hand to include the rise of mountains, the drought-touched fields, common in August, and the horse trailer tugging along behind them.

"So, no, I don't think it's a waste at all. Maybe, finally, I'm growing up."

Her words niggled that sore spot inside Jack. He'd had some growing up to do himself, and he'd fought it, but sitting alongside Liv, trailering horses and grabbing front-seat burgers, he felt as if he'd melded the old with the new into something wonderful.

Go slow. You messed with her head once. Treat her like you'll treat that horse behind you. Nice and gentle, with tender loving care. Horses and people who've been burned spook easy.

Jack pulled into the restaurant's parking lot and aligned the trailer beneath the shade of a tall, mature tree. He hopped out of the driver's seat, then turned. "Be right back. Don't go anywhere."

Her smile assured him she wouldn't, a smile he remembered well and couldn't believe how good it felt to see again. "I'll be right here, cowboy."

He tipped his brim and watched her smile deepen before heading inside. Their order was ready, just as Liv planned. To some, that might seem to be a minor thing, letting horses stand, trailered, while the owners ate.

Not to Livvie, and that said "rancher" all the way. She'd been gone a long time, yet she still carried that indefinable "ranch first" mentality, a rare trait that said she belonged in Big Sky country.

Seeing her sitting in the cab of the truck, busily

adding to her electronic notes when he came back through the restaurant door, his heart stretched open. She scrambled to stow the notepad as he climbed into the driver's seat. He handed off the bag and grinned at how deftly she distributed the food, the drinks, not a motion wasted, treating the front seat like a kitchen, cups here, napkins there, an old towel she'd found behind the seat draped over her lap to avoid drips from a well-topped and messy burger. He reached over and took her hand gently before they dived into the food.

She looked up. Saw his intent. Surprise faded to understanding and she squeezed his fingers lightly. "Go ahead."

He wanted to thank God for her. For this moment, this chance to set things right after too much time gone by. Would that embarrass her?

Maybe. He kept it short and sweet instead, but his heart rounded out the quick prayer. "God, thank You for this food. For the chance to be together, and Lord, we ask You to help us be the friends this gelding truly needs. To anticipate his needs until he feels safe and beloved once more. Amen."

She didn't let go of his hand straightaway, and that tiny measure of trust made him feel better. She held his gaze, her blue eyes almost misty, then smiled. "Thank you, Jack. That was lovely."

"You're lovely," he told her, letting his grin say the rest. "Let's see how lovely you stay while eating a big, sloppy ol' burger."

She popped down the hinge of his glove compartment to use as a miniature table, but the dust dissuaded her. She puffed it away, waved her hand and sent him a look that said he should clean the truck more often.

"I'll clean it this week. Promise. You know how bad the dust gets in July and August. And there's no keeping it out of the truck when I wear it into the truck multiple times a day."

"I hear you, cowboy. And a little dust ain't never been no big thing in these here parts," she drawled, teasing. "The fact that I'm sitting here about to eat one of the best burgers in all of Montana has me too happy to care." She followed that by taking her first bite, laughing when condiments slid one way while her burger seemed determined to go the other.

Too happy to care.

Her words brightened everything about the day. Words he reflected inside, a new joy taking hold, simply by spending a day with Livvie Franklin by his side. Talking horse, chatting baseball. Stealing quick, sideways glances.

Oh, yeah. Her words held true for both of them. Tucked inside the truck, angled so the horse trailer caught the shade from a broad, old maple tree while he and Liv roasted in the hot August sun?

Yup. Like Liv, he was too happy to care. And that felt better than he'd felt in a long time.

Chapter Five

Liv's conscience scolded nonstop the next day. If her brain was an iTune, she'd press Pause and move on, but the common-sense mental directives made her question her quick decisions at the livestock sale. By midday she had the downstairs polished, and headed to town to mosey around the library archives for a change of scenery. Chauncey Hardman took it upon herself to open the library for a few hours every Sunday afternoon, and there were times when getting lost in research could prove beneficial. She hoped that method worked today. Then she'd face a late-day dinner at the ranch with Jack, Coach and the horses. Hanging with Jack yesterday, she remembered how much she loved all three.

She turned down Shaw Boulevard, angled into the library lot and parked alongside a metallic blue hybrid, a sweet ride that said "money" despite its diminutive size. For just a moment Liv considered moving her worn, red Neon to the other side of the narrow lot, but that might insult the trusty old car, so she gave the slightly dented trunk a pat and a promise of a car wash as she headed inside.

The one-story library had little seating, but that didn't matter today. Liv turned to the right, down a short hall, and straight into the history section of the converted ranch-style house, a small space that had probably been a bedroom at one time. The square room now housed all historical nonfiction on one wall and fiction on the other. Chauncey had her own way of doing things and since the Hardmans had bequeathed their house to the library thirty-five years before, no one was about to argue with the stout middle-aged librarian.

"Oh. Hey. Sorry."

A slim woman with long blond hair swung around as Liv drew up short.

Liv made a face and tapped the doorway. "Didn't see you with the turn and there's never anyone back here when I come in to work. Hi."

The other woman smiled and swept the small room a look of understanding. "It's kind of fun and odd how small this is, isn't it?" She extended her hand and said, "I'm Robin Frazier. I'm staying in town for a little while and I love to check out old stuff."

"Then you've come to the right room," Liv noted. As she grasped Robin's offered hand, her gaze fell on the leather-bound document spread out on the table behind Robin. "The Shaw history. I was going through that myself the other day. Find anything interesting?"

"Not much."

The woman looked almost disappointed, as if she'd been hoping to find some deep dark secret hidden in the old parchment papers. Livvie was pretty sure that if such a thing existed, Jackson Shaw would have prettied it up—or excised it. Jackson had a way of gilding things with his own special spin, not a quality Liv admired, especially from a historical perspective. How could people learn from the mistakes of a spit-shined past that didn't reflect reality? "Were you looking for something specific?"

"No." Robin answered too quickly, but before Liv could wonder at her speedy response, she went on, "I'm working on my degree and doing a thesis on genealogy. Documenting family histories is part of the process."

"I love history, fact and fiction," Liv admitted. "Austen, Brontë, Alcott. I look at the early women novelists and there's a part of me that wishes I could see romance and life the way they did."

Robin laughed out loud. "Washing clothes in wooden tubs and wringing them out by hand while stringing green beans into 'leather britches'?"

"Those images do take the sheen off the romance," Liv admitted. She was about to say something else, when Chauncey stepped into the room, a hand braced on one broad hip while her other held a pointer finger to her lips.

"A library, ladies, not a coffee shop. Whisper, please."

Liv peeked around the corner, then faced Chauncey. "But there's no one else here, Mrs. Hardman."

"That doesn't mean someone couldn't walk in that door at any moment, young lady. Rules are rules." She waggled two thick eyebrows at the younger women, and while she didn't look exactly displeased, Liv was pretty sure her demeanor meant "conversation: over." She turned to face Robin again. "Do you want to talk about the Jasper Gulch history some more? The diner's open around the corner."

"I'd love it." Robin began to hoist the heavy history volume, but Chauncey tsk-tsked that idea.

"I'll do it, I've got it, don't trouble yourself. These old volumes take a special touch." She clapped the book shut and placed it on the shelf with a firm thump that meant business. "Anytime you need one of those specials, you ring me. I'll be glad to get it for you. If I'm not busy, of course."

"Of course." Robin smiled at the older woman and didn't seem put off by Chauncey's gruff manner. "Lovers of history must stick together."

Chauncey beamed a smile on her that included Liv as they moved to the door, and Liv was pretty sure she'd taken a firm step up in the librarian's estimation, just because Robin smiled at the right time. A good lesson to learn when dealing with die-hard residents of Jasper Gulch. And not such a difficult one to follow.

"Should we drive over or leave the cars here?" Robin wondered as they moved down the three steps to the short sidewalk linking the asphalt lot to the Western-style library.

"We can leave them. It's hot, but it's a short walk. Oh." Liv followed the direction of Robin's gaze to the long chain wrapped around a thick, metal pole at the parking lot entrance. "You think Chauncey's going to close that gate, right?"

"I assumed so, at closing time. I take it she's not going to do that?"

Liv grinned and set off for Main Street, and as they passed the chain she pointed north. "Chauncey Hardman only closes this parking lot during the rodeo and round-up weekends. She says she won't have any foul beasts contaminating her lot with their droppings so when there are horses and trailers moving around the business district, Chauncey puts up her chain."

"But it's asphalt." Robin looked at the small lot and then back to Liv. "Couldn't it just be rinsed off with a hose? Horses are a part of life in Jasper Gulch, right?"

"As much as anything else, yes. But Chauncey's mother rode off with a rodeo rider about fifty years ago and never looked back. Chauncey's had nothing to do with horses ever since."

"But she stayed." Robin's expression said something didn't compute. "She stayed in a place that's surrounded by horses and cattle ranches. That doesn't make sense."

"It does if you love Big Sky country. And Chauncey Hardman, for all her idiosyncrasies, loves Montana, heart and soul. She does the greatest history exhibit in the fall and a living-history pageant every spring in the park. I think I fell in love with history listening to Chauncey weave stories when I was a kid, but I know better than to ask her about horses…"

"Duly noted," Robin said with a laugh.

"And to talk in her library."

"Lesson learned." Robin followed Liv into the old-style cross-buck door of Great Gulch Grub, the hometown café. Empty tables filled the middle with the lunch crowd long gone, while booths lined the outer walls. They settled into a booth close to the short counter. Robin sat back and swept the retro-Western interior a look of appreciation. "Every time I stop in here, I feel like I'm walking onto a movie set. The punched-tin ceiling, the wagon-wheel lights, the old, worn floor."

"And I love that fifty-plus years of wipe-downs has dulled the finish on half of the tables. I wouldn't have it any other way." Liv smiled as the middle-aged daytime waitress swaggered their way. "Mert,

I'd love a coffee, and if you put a shot of caramel in it, I'd die happy."

"With Granny's fresh rice pudding?" Mert wondered.

"Rice, milk, eggs..." Liv pretended to ponder. "That sounds healthy to me. Robin, you won't be sorry if you order the rice pudding, it's an old family recipe that no one shares—"

Mert tapped the worn tabletop with a bright blue freshly polished fingernail. "If everybody and his brother has the recipe, why in the name of Sam Hill would they come here to get it? Business savvy." She bestowed a humor-filled look of wisdom to Robin and Liv, then nodded Robin's way. "And you like your coffee without the froufrou stuff Livvie asks for and I expect Granny's fresh peach pie would sit right for a Sunday afternoon."

"With vanilla ice cream, I'm a happy woman," declared Robin.

"You're in here fairly often, then." Liv turned her attention back to Robin and jerked a thumb toward Mert's retreating back. "To have Mert know your likes."

"Well, she's smart as a whip and I figured that out the first day in." Robin nodded to an older fellow who passed their table on his way out. "And she likes her customers happy. I found that to be true with a lot of the folks in this town."

"But not all."

Robin gave Liv a look of consideration, then

shrugged. "I haven't been here long enough to have opinions, not really."

Liv snorted because Jasper Gulch was great, but like any small town, it had its share of snippy folks.

Robin acknowledged the sound with a smile and a nod. "Okay, there are a few interesting characters, but mostly folks are charming. And totally Western. I didn't realize how different things were here until I got here."

Liv considered her words, thought a moment, then asked, "Didn't realize? Like you knew about Jasper Gulch before you came? But we're not big enough or notable enough to bring folks in unless they're fishing or hunting, Robin. And you're not here to do either. And it's not like our history here is core-curriculum stuff. We weren't on any cutting edge of anything historical and we've stayed small, except for the size of the ranches, and pretty much unchanged and to ourselves for generations. So having you come here, curious about history, kind of makes me curious about you."

Robin's face said one thing. Her words? Quite another. "I had stuff I needed to get away from. Nothing hugely bad, just stuff. I wanted to head west, see how things work here, and maybe find the roots my family lost a long time ago. I got here just in time for the rodeo, but then the huge celebration for the time capsule turned into a complete bust because it was stolen. And then someone intentionally started a fire at the rodeo. Even though it got caught quickly and put out, that made me wonder what kind of town Jasper Gulch really is."

"Usually good, quiet and peaceful," Liv declared. "I don't think anyone remembers a time when you couldn't just do as you would, doors unlocked. Right now folks are worried. You can see that in their faces. As to the past?" She shrugged. "A lot of folks stopped here then moved on. The mountains are tough for some, there was little in the way of business opportunity because the town avoided change, and water rights make everybody a little crazy. So we've had our share of folks who leave in search of easier ways. But having said all that…." Liv leaned back and waved toward the wide double windows facing Main Street. "I fell in love with Jasper Gulch all over again when I came back nearly two weeks ago. I didn't fully appreciate what a great place this was until I got a taste of other things. Now I have to weigh all that up." Liv reached up and accepted her caramel coffee from Mert with a smile of thanks. "With jobs scarce and not much new, I have no idea if there's a plausible reason for staying here."

"I can think of one available cowboy who could help you with that dilemma, Liv Franklin. But I don't expect you'll be wantin' advice in that particular arena."

"Thank you, no." Liv sent Mert a look that said her assumption was spot-on. "Single and staying that way is my current mantra."

"Time's got a way of changin' those mantra things when we least expect it," Mert advised. She gave a knowing look out the front door as a Shaw truck rumbled past, and when she looked back at Liv, her smile smacked of wisdom. "When Julie Shaw came strollin' in here last month, leadin' that rodeo cowboy around like a ring-nosed bull, I knew right off where that pair was headed. Straight to the altar, and I'm rarely wrong about things like that after livin' in these parts for my share of decades. But you take your time, Livvie. Jack McGuire's not goin' anywhere. Not with those new horses you and he bought yesterday."

And there it was, the single most important reason for hightailing it out of Jasper Gulch and burying herself in another city.

Everyone here knew about her and Jack and everyone and their mother expected them to form some kind of Hollywood movie-set bond because they both happened to be back in town at the same time. Single. Loving horses. And a little nostalgic with her biological clock ticking away.

Robin straightened her shoulders and perked up. "Is Jack cute? And nice? And a churchgoer? Because if Liv's not in the market for a smokin'-hot cowboy, I sure am."

Liv burst out laughing. So did Mert. And Robin looked pleased with herself for easing Liv's growing tension. "I'm going to warn you off, but not because I have any designs on Jack myself."

Mert snorted as she dished up a very generous helping of ice cream to Robin's peach pie on her side of the counter.

"But because it would be real nice to be able to have a conversation with one person in this town—" Liv raised her voice just enough for Mert to hear and appreciate in the otherwise empty restaurant "—that doesn't play matchmaker with me and Jack McGuire."

"We could make a pact."

The distinctly male voice behind Liv made her heart crunch and her pulse spike. "Where did you come from? Because you weren't behind me a minute ago."

Jack tipped his hat to Robin, squatted low and eyed the rice pudding Mert set down in front of Liv, and his grin widened when Mert used a little more gusto than necessary to top the pudding with thick whipped cream. "You're not spoiling your appetite for supper, are you?"

Robin smiled.

Mert grinned an "I told you so" look that would spread around town like a late-summer wildfire by nightfall.

"Actually, I—"

"Coach is excited to see you," Jack interrupted as if she hadn't been about to offer objections. "And we need to catch up on the baseball history and game stuff we never got to yesterday, once we had the horses."

True, but—

"Do you want to drive out to the ranch, or can I pick you up?"

"Pick her up," Mert advised, her face showing approval because picking a girl up sounded like a date.

"I'll drive, of course." Liv scolded Mert with a look, but the middle-aged woman just laughed and went back to stocking the counter for the Monday-morning crowd. "Jack, this is Robin Frazier. She's in town to do some Montana history."

"Something you know a lot about and you two have in common."

"So it seems." Robin smiled at him, and Liv wasn't afraid to send her a look that said while Jack wasn't exactly "taken," he wasn't one bit available, either.

"Are you here in town?" Jack asked and Robin nodded.

"I'm at Mamie Fidler's place, and between Mamie, Mert and now Chauncey, I don't have to go very far to find exactly the kind of characters I love to read about. Funny, smart, sassy, down-home folks with good hearts."

"Don't forget nosey."

Robin burst out laughing. So did Mert. And as Jack stood, he reached out a hand and quick-grabbed the bill for their coffee and dessert. "This one's on me, ladies."

"Jack, I—"

"It's the least I can do for my new ranch hand, right?" His look toward Mert assured she heard and approved as she handed him a white to-go sack. When she grinned, he went on, "I'll see you later, okay? Around six? I headed into town because I heard that Granny had made fresh rice pudding and how a certain someone has a particular fondness for that dessert." He lofted the bag. "Twice in one day, Liv. That can't be bad. So. See you at six?"

He'd driven to town to buy some of Granny's rice pudding for their dessert because someone—Mert, no doubt—had called to advise him. Talk about sweet. And to-die-for good-looking. She waved him out the door but didn't hide the tiny smile of satisfaction his trip wrought. "Yes. Fine. Go. You've stirred up enough trouble for one day, Jack."

He smiled, said goodbye to Mert and didn't look back, most likely because he knew all three women would be watching him go. And when he'd cleared the door by less than a foot, Mert refilled their coffee, smiled down at Liv and said easily, "I'm not saying a word to anyone about this, Liv, and there's one very good reason for that."

"And that is?" Liv raised her gaze to the waitress's wise eyes.

"It's too important this time, and I don't want to see anything so sweet, nice and downright good get messed up again. And that's the whole of it."

Livvie wanted to hug her, but Mert wasn't the hugging sort, except this time, it was Mert who leaned down and put a quick arm around Liv's shoulders. "Welcome home, Liv."

Her words touched Liv's heart and possibly her soul. Maybe the town wasn't just bored and addled with minding everyone's business. Maybe… like Robin said…most folks were just plain nice, looking out for each other. And that made a world of difference.

Chapter Six

"I grabbed a couple of extra steaks to throw on the fire," Mick McGuire announced as Jack climbed out of the truck later that afternoon. "And washed up a few more potatoes."

"Because?"

A shout of laughter pulled Jack's attention left. Two school-age kids romped in a clean hay pile that hadn't existed that morning. The barn ladder gave them easy access to the pile, and then they jumped, tumbling down the pale green heap, landing and laughing at the bottom.

"Mick, would you like more tea?"

Jack turned, spotted the nice-looking woman at the side porch door and sent his father a look of interest that made the older man color up. "That's Carrie."

"Hmm." Jack smiled as the woman crossed the yard. Before she got close enough to hear, he stepped closer to his father. "Reason to whistle right there."

He expected his father to grow more embarrassed, but Mick surprised him by just nodding and thrusting his hands deep into his pockets. "Yes, it is."

Mick's simple reply caught Jack up short. If he'd laughed it off, Jack could have minimized his father's interest in the fortyish woman heading their way. But a quick agreement? And the smile he bestowed as the woman approached with two tall glasses of tea?

That said more than his sparse words ever could. "I'm Jack." He stuck out a hand and the woman eyed the tea, his hand, laughed and passed a glass to Mick, flashing him a look as she did, a look they shared for a quick, bright moment.

"Carrie Landry. And that's Maggie." She pointed to the pig-tailed tomboy scrambling up the barnside ladder as if born to climb. "And Brian. Mick invited us to supper, but then he saw your stuff laid out and realized you might be having company. I hope it's not an intrusion, Jack. We can always come another night."

"Nonsense." Mick waved it off as if a house full of company was the norm, and it had been, back in the day. When Mom was alive and folks stopped by all hours of the day for coffee, sweet tea and honest answers about most anything. "We love a crowd."

"It's fine, really." Jack followed his father's cue as the kids raced their way, shrieking about how cool the ranch was. "Coach is coming by for a steak roast."

"It'll be good to see him." Mick picked up Maggie and swung her high into the air, settling her on his shoulders, a move Jack remembered from his own childhood.

"And Livvie."

His father paused, nodded and almost smiled. "Good to see her, too. I expect there's a story behind the livestock that showed up in the front barn yesterday."

"With women, there's always a story, isn't there?"

"Truth to tell, son." Mick sent Carrie a teasing look, then shifted his attention to the fire pit. "You want to get the fire going or should I?"

"You take the kids—"

"I'm Maggie!" The little girl caroled the words from Mick's broad shoulders as if onstage. "I'm five and I'm in kindergarten but they're moving me to first grade because I already know everything."

"Good to know." Jack reached up and shook the girl's hand, and wasn't surprised when she offered a wicked-strong handshake for a little kid. "And you're Brian. I expect you're a bit older than your noisy sister, eh?" Jack smiled and squatted to lessen the height difference. "Eight years old?"

"No, sir. Seven."

"Well, you look eight," Jack declared. "Obviously mature for your age."

A small shy smile told Jack he'd done well,

but then the boy glanced down, kicked the dirt, scrubbed his toe into the tiny divot he'd made and shrugged. "I'm just seven, though."

The horses nickered behind the barn. One whinnied, then another followed suit before they dashed across the new paddock as if they owned the place. The boy shrank back. His actions pushed Jack to offer a different plan. "Brian, do you want to help me start the fire? I'd be glad for some company."

"Sure. Can I?" He turned his face up toward his mother, imploring.

"*May* I," his mother corrected him, but then she nodded. When she lifted her gaze to Jack, she sent him a silent look of gratitude. "And yes, but follow Jack's directions, okay?"

"I will."

"I like fires," Maggie announced. "But I like horses more. I want to know everything there is to know about horses, Mr. Mick. Like everything in the world. Is that okay?" She leaned down, a totally fearless move because one wrong shift of her weight would send her tumbling over Mick McGuire's broad shoulders. Not that Jack's father was about to let that happen. He held firm to her legs and shrugged affably. "I can teach you all I know. And that's a fair bit."

"Then that's perfect," she declared, righting herself. "When I grow up I want to run a ranch like this. I want to ride horses all day and night. I want—"

Mick put a finger to his lips and turned his gaze up. "The first thing to know about horses is this. They like quiet voices. Easy movements. We don't want to spook them. Or scare them. Or hurt their ears. They're big, but they're sensitive."

"Like you, Mr. Mick!" Maggie took his cue and said the words softly, but her enthusiasm didn't wane with the loss of volume. "I'll talk soft and steady, just like you taught me."

"Good enough."

Hearing his father coach a small child on the ins and outs of horse training, Jack pitched back two dozen years to when he rode Mick's shoulders into the barn. In those twenty-four years his father had offered a full education in horse mastery. Jack had learned at the feet and then the side of one of the best wranglers in the West, and seeing him now, with the five-year-old perched on his shoulders...?

The image hit Jack twofold. Life would go on without his mother, just as she'd promised him before she passed away.

But it would go on different, and watching his father stride toward the corral, snugging the little girl's legs against his chest and chatting with Carrie as she carried two glasses of homemade sweet tea, made him realize things could be changing around the Double M, in more ways than one. And he wasn't sure how to feel about any of that.

"Mr. Jack?"

The boy's tug at his waist drew Jack's attention. "Caught me out, kid. I was daydreaming, wasn't I?"

The boy's serious nod said he was, but that it was okay.

Jack grabbed a wheelbarrow, then the boy, tucked the startled child into the wheelbarrow and rode him across the barnyard to the stacks of firewood seasoning in the sun. When he dumped Brian out, the boy laughed up at him, a little looser than he'd been minutes before. They piled wood high into the barrow, big wood first, then kindling on top, and when they were ready to tote the load over to the fire pit, Brian looked up. "Can I help push?"

"I'd be obliged," admitted Jack, and he tamed the threatening smile as the boy positioned himself in front of Jack, hands on the twin poles. "Ready?"

Brian fisted both poles, puckered his face in concentration and nodded. "Yes, sir."

Polite. Nice. Quiet. Unsure.

The boy's actions said there was a story inside him, but right now, with Jack's help, he concentrated his efforts on moving wood across the long expanse of barnyard and driveway to the McGuire fire pit behind the house. And when they pulled up alongside the pit, satisfaction marked the boy's expression. He set the wheelbarrow onto its legs, released the poles and scrubbed the palms of his hands against his thighs. "What next?"

"We build." Jack pointed to a small pile of dry grass clippings to the left of the house.

"Grass, then kindling?"

"You've started fires before."

"My dad and me used to do this. A long time ago."

Jack's heart tightened. The boy's joy faded in the shadow of a tough memory. Jack understood that emotion but kept things light. "Well, then, it's good to have experience on our side, right? Grab me a pile of those clippings and we'll get this fire going."

"'Kay."

Within minutes they had a lovely kindling fire burning, and Jack coached Brian on how to gently place the logs into the heat, not throw them.

"It's easier to toss 'em," Brian noted. He eyed the fire with due respect. "It's hot when you get too close."

"It is and I'll do it if you'd rather," Jack offered. He pointed toward the hay lots surrounding the house and the forested ridge beyond. "Fires in late summer can be dangerous. If it's windy or too dry, we use the outdoor grill because one little spark can set off a blaze that takes down a forest."

Brian's gulp said he knew that, but then he sucked in a breath, crept closer and gently rolled a split piece of wood onto the fire. "How was that?"

"Perfect. Now you need two more."

The boy did the extra two pieces with care, watching as he rolled the split logs from the built-up stone wall into the campfire area below. "We let these burn for a little while," Brian whispered as if repeating directions. "Then add more."

"Exactly." Jack squatted low and swept the fire pit a glance. "You know a lot about the basics of fire building. How'd you get to be so smart, kid? Are you a Boy Scout?"

"No, sir." Brian stared at the fire, sighed, then drew his gaze back to Jack, but the look on his face, as if he'd just met a monster head-on, broke Jack's heart. "My dad was a firefighter. He was in Hose Company 7 when they dropped into the Crimson Ridge fire two years ago."

Crimson Ridge. The forest fire in central Idaho that called in units for a five-hundred-mile radius. The fire that surrounded an ace team of firefighters, taking the lives of seven men within minutes. This boy had lost his father in the line of duty, a man who'd made his living protecting others.

Reality broadsided Jack. He'd been wallowing around, a full-grown man, floundering for too long because he'd lost his baseball career, then his mom.

This little guy had lost his father at an age when memories would fade with time. An age when a boy needs a dad, a living example, a big, strong guy with a gentle voice to build a kid's confidence and ego.

A light whistle sounded from the barn area, an old kids' tune, and when Maggie picked up on the song and started wailing about workin' on a railroad, Jack's heart softened. His gut relaxed.

"'Prosper the work of our hands for us. Prosper the work of our hands,'" Jack said.

If being here on this ranch with the McGuires helped this young family and maybe led to something else, something of a more permanent nature, then maybe that's what God intended. His thoughts went back to the morning service and Ethan's advice to live each day on purpose.

He needed to do that more.

Liv hadn't shown up in church. Maybe she'd gone to one of the smaller churches in town. Or maybe she'd avoided him and services and slept in.

A small red car wound its way toward the ranch from the north. A white van sporting the Bobcats baseball logo followed not far behind. Jack squatted and indicated his shoulders. "Hop on. We've got some old friends to greet."

"Really?" Brian's face lit up at the thought of riding high on Jack's shoulders. "I'm not too big?"

Jack shot him a look that said "as if," and Brian scrambled onto his broad shoulders without waiting for a second invite. And when Coach Randolph and Liv both smiled their way moments later, the thought of old friends and new acquaintances mingling together on an August evening seemed mighty fine.

"Those kids are adorable." Liv cut a slab of triple-chocolate cake and laid it on Coach's plate alongside a scoop of Granny's rice pudding later that evening. "If your doctor takes issue with this, it's not my fault, Coach."

"I'll be especially good the rest of the week," the big man told her in a James Earl Jones–type voice. "And as for you, Livvie Franklin, it does my heart good to see you back home here, for however long. We've fallen on some tough times hereabouts, not too many jobs available and some shenanigans going on, but it does this old heart good to see some of our young people return."

"Well, gainful employment is a tough go around here." Liv whacked off another hunk of cake for Jack before giving herself a serving of the rice pudding Jack had gone into town to buy. Just for her. That thought warmed her. But she'd keep Jack at a safe distance no matter how much she loved Granny's desserts. Better all around. "A girl can't live with Mom and Dad forever. Still, the timing is oddly correct. Mom called today to say Grandma and Grandpa are moving here. I think I can be a help to them. Or at least a buffer."

"They need help?" The timbre of Coach's voice shifted deeper.

"Grandpa has Alzheimer's. Grandma kept hoping it was something else, but I guess that's wishful thinking now."

"Liv, I'm sorry." Jack's expression said he meant the words. "If there's anything we can do to help, just let me know."

She slanted a wistful smile up to him as they

moved toward the fire. Carrie, Mick and the kids had already feasted on dessert and moved straight into toasting marshmallows on long, thin sticks. "Thanks. I'm going to take it day by day. None of us has any experience, so—" she lifted her shoulders and made a face of acceptance "—we'll see."

"I have always believed life happens for a reason, even if that logic is hard for us to find." Coach pointed skyward. "Now, Him, the Good Lord, He's got himself a mighty fine vantage point and He sees! Oh, yes, He sees. And did you folks know that Major League Baseball now hosts an Alzheimer's Awareness Day in September?" Coach settled into a spot on one of the broad, wooden benches. "Folks wear purple to support funding and research."

"Well, I've been in a bubble, it seems, because I honestly knew little about Alzheimer's until Mom mentioned it last week," Livvie confessed. "On top of that, I hadn't visited my grandparents in five years, and I'm pretty ashamed of myself right now."

Mick raised a blazing marshmallow, puffed air over it, then shifted his gaze to her. "Life gets busy. And we get caught up in the day-to-day. Sometimes we just forget to appreciate what's around us until it's gone, but that doesn't make us bad people, Liv."

"But it surely can make us more aware," Coach added. He set his cake plate down and leaned back on the bench. "When Gladys was alive, we had such plans, such dreams for retirement. Neither one of us had a notion of not being here to enjoy it.

We thought of things to do over the winters, places to go once the baseball season wound down mid-fall." He shrugged forward and clasped his hands together. "But I don't let myself think of what we missed, uh-uh. I focus on what we had." He emphasized the last word with a firm nod. "Nearly thirty years together. Now, *that's* something! Two fine kids who go to church regular and raise their youngsters right. Three sweet grandsons and another baby on the way, a little girl this time. When I look at what we have versus what I've lost, I realize the Lord's been mighty good to me. Why, this cake alone is worth a round of the 'Hallelujah Chorus'!"

Carrie laughed out loud. "Well, thank you, Coach. And as much fun as this has been—" she aimed a pointed look at the two kids "—we have to go. I have work in the morning and Maggie and Brian need to finish up their last week of summer camp."

"Couldn't we just do camp here?" Maggie added charm to the wheedling tone of voice by tilting her head back to catch Mick's eye. "You have horses and cows and woods and water and maybe you've even got crayons. I think we should just make our summer camp here, Mr. Mick."

Mick smiled down at her, eased to his feet with her still in his arms, then stepped away from the fire to toss her over his shoulder in a fireman's hold. "Nice try, kid. When Mom tells us what to do…?"

Maggie huffed out an overdone sigh with a hand flourish to deepen the dramatic effect. "We do it."

"Bingo. How many stars do you see, Mags?"

The little girl craned her neck as Mick eased her into a more upright position. "So many. So very many. Like a bajillion, at least."

Brian stood and yawned before stepping away from the fire. At the corner of the squared-off stone patio he turned back. "Hey, Jack. Thanks for letting me help."

He didn't look at the fire, but Jack read the emotion behind the words. Such a little guy to carry so much woe. "You did good, bud. You did good."

The boy's gaze locked with Jack's and they both understood the deeper meaning behind the praise.

"Liv, Coach, nice meeting you. You, too, Jack, and thanks for taking Brian under your wing." Carrie settled an easy hand around the boy's shoulders. "He gets tired of girl talk."

"Then bring him around more often." Jack jerked his head toward the house behind them. "With cake like that, I wouldn't mind having you guys stop by regular."

Carrie met his gaze. Seemed to read his meaning. And in the dancing light of fire-pit flames, he was pretty sure she blushed, but maybe the pink in her cheeks was from the heat of the fire. She glanced up, saw Mick's smile and ducked her head slightly. And this time Jack was certain the blush had nothing to do with the ebbing campfire. Quietly, she and Mick moved toward her car with the two tired kids, cricket chatter murmuring through the human silence.

"You did okay." Coach broke the quiet as he set his plate aside and stood, nodding in the direction of Jack's dad. "But I've got an early day tomorrow, too, then a week of play-offs coming up. If you've got time to do some batting and field practice with my boys, I'd appreciate it."

Coach had asked before, and each time he did, Jack had refused politely, avoiding baseball at all costs. Now he saw the childish aspects of his former actions and stood. "What time?"

A spark of approval brightened Coach's face. "Four-thirty. We're using the fields in Ennis because the slope's different and I wanna change things up a little."

"See you then."

"Miss Livvie? Good night."

"Night, Coach."

Jack turned her way as Coach strode toward his van. "Pretty nice, this." He shifted his attention to the fire, then the sky. "A pretty girl, a campfire and a bajillion stars."

"Except, while I'm a woman of too much leisure at the moment, you've got to get up at dawn and ride herd. Or something like that."

Jack laughed because they'd just repastured the herd, but he would be up early, caring for animals, then shifting hay to winter quarters with a couple of hands once the dew dried. As summer wound down, each task done put a rancher one step ahead of Mother Nature's eventual onslaught. "Plenty of work, for sure. And we didn't get much planning done today, Liv. I'm sorry about that."

She stood, dusted off the seat of her pants and shook her head. "I'm not. I had a great time, it was nice to just sit and relax with great people. I can't remember the last time I let myself sit and chat with no work involved."

Neither could Jack, and the reality surprised him. "It seems like we both need to get out more. Probably not much harm in doing some of that together."

Liv put her hand up, fingers spread. "Stop right there, cowboy. I put you in the off-limits category years ago. You might think you're ready to be upgraded, but I'm not so sure, and I've got a hefty to-do list right now, including getting this town history accomplished. While it might seem like I've got plenty of time, not everyone's as forthcoming about Jasper Gulch's historical roots as Chet and Let Shaw seem to have been. I keep stumbling on gaps with very little said, and for a fairly recent history, you'd think my task would be easy." She made a face as they walked to her car. "But it's not, and that tweaks my interest. Why are there gaps? And who benefits from them?"

"Not everybody's inclined to write down history, Liv." Jack shrugged when they arrived at her car door. "Couldn't it be that simple?"

"It could," she admitted. "But the gaps are spaced in such a way that some of them are in the early days of the town and others are around the time of Lucy Shaw's death. As if someone deliberately left things out or removed pages to change the look of the town's history."

"Who would do that?" Jack asked, then went on to the more obvious question for a non-history buff. "Who'd care?"

"See, that's it, Jack. Most people don't embrace history like I do, so when things go missing or spaces of time disappear, the average person wouldn't know or care. But I got a call today from the mayor himself."

"Because?"

Liv scrunched up her face in annoyance. "It seems the council received a note."

"A note?" Jack frowned, not understanding. "About what?" The idea of passing notes seemed pretty adolescent to him.

"'If you want to know what happened to your time-capsule, you need to think about L.S.,'" Liv quoted.

Jack pretended to clean out his ears. "Say what?"

"Exactly. Now the council wants me to study any and all things that might give them clues about why the capsule might have been stolen. What was in it that brought someone's attention. And then the mayor asked me point-blank to keep an eye on Lilibeth Shoemaker because she might be involved."

"Only if the capsule harbored makeup and shoes," Jack supposed. "Why would they target a girl like Lilibeth? It— Ah. The initials."

"L.S.," Liv confirmed. "But you're right, there is no reason to think Lilibeth would have anything to do with digging up a time capsule."

"Getting dirty," Jack deadpanned.

The truth of his words lightened Liv's expression. "That sums it up, right there. Lilibeth might be self-serving and obnoxious, but she's young. Silly. And she doesn't get her hands dirty for anything. I'm kind of amazed she's working at the ice-cream parlor, but it does give her proximity to all of the Middletons' customer base, and single, cute guys need food. In Lilibeth's world, that's a simple equation. Anyway, Jackson and Abigail Rose at the town hall want me to hunt for anything buried in the capsule that might have caught Lilibeth's eye."

"A prospect for a rich husband?" Jack wondered, but the quest about Lilibeth made him further question the sensibilities involved. "No one in their right mind would suspect Lilibeth of being involved in anything more than borrowing her sisters' clothes. Although with three girls in the house, that might be considered a capital offense."

Livvie's grin rewarded him.

"I'll think about it, too," he promised. Of course he'd think about it, because he didn't like Liv's look of worry. Her furrowed brow. He'd made a pledge to make her smile again. Hear her laugh more often.

This was a chance to meet that goal. "And I don't put much worth in anonymous notes, Liv. If someone knows something, he or she should have the gumption to just say it outright."

"Maybe they're scared?"

"Here? Really?" A crazy thought, right until Jack matched up the intentionally set fire at the rodeo. Maybe the note writer was worried for good reason, even in Jasper Gulch. "We might all have to take this stuff more seriously. The capsule theft. The fire. The gaps in the history."

"Well, I'm pretty sure the council didn't expect these gaps. I've got to give them my initial report next week, and explain that someone may have been doctoring the town's historical records. I think it's too much of a coincidence to not be related to the capsule theft," she admitted. She shifted her gaze to meet his. "The capsule's missing and so are parts of Jasper Gulch's history. And now this note, unsigned. I think it's pretty clear that the stuff going on is linked somehow. But I can't think how or why."

Right now it was hard to think at all, looking down into Liv's blue eyes. Her face, half-shadowed, reminded him of all the times they'd stood like this, saying goodbye at the end of an evening. The sweetness of her face, the earnest look in her eyes, the curve of her cheek in the sweep of barnyard light.

He reached one hand to her cheek, just to see if

the skin he remembered as if it was yesterday was still as soft and sweet.

Yup.

And was it his imagination, or did she turn her face into the palm of his hand for one quick second, letting him cradle the curve of smooth, feminine skin?

But then she straightened, stepped back, sent him a scolding look and tsk-tsked him with her finger. "Knock it off."

He smiled, knowing she wasn't putting too much sting into the reprimand as he opened the car door for her. "I didn't promise, remember? I merely said I understood the rules."

The look on her face said she remembered, all right, but as she offered him a pretend frown through the driver's-side window, he saw something else, something that nearly brought him to his knees, begging forgiveness.

A sheen of tears, blinked back.

Nothing major, Liv had never been a crier, but he knew what he saw. His gesture, so sweet and good on his part, took her back to a broken heart she never should have had. His stupidity and stubbornness had created a chasm that couldn't be shrugged away because he was finally growing up enough to put things right in his world, mostly because it took him way too long.

He'd knocked her universe into disarray eight years before, and it would take more than a few bowls of rice pudding to set things right. But if God gave him time?

He'd do what he could.

Chapter Seven

You should be tucked in the center of downtown, squinting over scripted penmanship and wiping off dusty volumes of decades-old facts. What are you thinking, girlfriend?

Liv hauled in a deep breath, the scent of horse, hay and Big Sky drenching her.

This felt like home. A home she didn't dare long for, a home she'd written off long ago, but there was no denying that whenever she set foot onto the Double M, the place engulfed her like a cozy room on a winter's night.

Home is where the heart is.

Jack's mother had loved that saying and Liv had spent a lot of time talking with her back in the day. She'd learned horse husbandry at Mary Beth's side, the blend of gentle-to-firm so important with large animals.

At present, the young stallion was taking direction from Jack. He'd decided right off to take the young horse under his wing, urging and guiding him to Double M standards. The mares were set apart for a bit, long enough to make sure they weren't harboring anything dangerous to the rest of the herd, and caring for them was a simple task. Animals brought up with love just expected it along the way, and the mares were no exception.

But the buckskin, timid, tired and torn about whom to trust, was Liv's personal responsibility and she waited every morning until Jack should be out on the range before heading to the Double M.

Bawk! Bawk!

I'm not a chicken, she scolded her inner voice. I'd call it smart. Savvy. Avoiding conflict isn't cowardice, it's wise.

It's not conflict you're avoiding, her conscience returned. *It's emotion because you went moony-eyed when Jack cupped your cheek last week. And then you acted surprised by the old feelings it stirred, as if you'd ever gotten over him. Please. Let's play this straight, shall we?*

Liv shoved the inner scolding aside. She'd gotten over being dumped years ago. Hadn't she proved that by living in Chicago and ignoring Jack's presence? And then she'd moved on to a new life, a new job, a marriage. Proof enough right there.

The horse sighed as she smoothed the brush over his back in long, slow strokes. She was building confidence with him. And maybe with herself.

An engine rolled into the barnyard and Liv

paused, startled. Jack? Mick? Why would they be back here midmorning?

Two young voices shouted glee as Maggie and Brian Landry raced past the open barn framing the paddock's far edge. Carrie's caution sounded behind them, a reminder to calm down, go slow, lower their voices. She poked her head into the near paddock, spotted Liv and came her way. "I saw your car tucked on the far side of the barn and figured you were back here. How's he doing?"

"Better, maybe. It's hard to tell because his condition was so bad." Liv kept her voice crooning-low, comforting the gelding while answering Carrie, a trick Mary Beth McGuire had shared years back. "If we're on the right track, another two weeks should work wonders. And two months down the road? We should see him for who he really is."

"Amazing endurance," Carrie said softly. She watched the kids as they circled the far paddock, Maggie fearlessly perched on the bottom rail, chatting with the new mares, while Brian hung to the outside, watching. "I didn't used to think about things like that. Faith. Fortitude. Endurance. But when my husband died, I started to see things in a new light because I had to." She reached in and stroked the horse's face with a smooth touch. "I didn't realize I was kind of going through the motions of living until I got slapped upside the head with a dose of reality. Nothing like a total left turn to remind us how precious and tenuous life is. So much we take for granted."

Liv worked the brush over the horse's hindquarters, keeping her touch light. Hints of new hair growth along his flank said the upgraded diet was starting to take effect. "It had to be hard." She turned her gaze toward the two children, a summer picture of Montana ranch life. "To lose someone you love and become a single parent overnight. How do you manage, Carrie?"

Carrie's smile said the answer was obvious. "God. Faith. Time. Healing. Once I got over being mad, crazy overprotective of the kids and fairly self-defeating, I realized life offers us opportunities all the time. But it doesn't come with guarantees, so I took off my blinders and grabbed hold of the reins. My husband was a good man, a wonderful father and he had a heart of gold. But he laughed in the face of God, shrugging off faith as a nonessential entity." She grimaced, remembering, then paused and called out a soft caution to Maggie.

"He'd quote scientific jargon to minimize God's reality," she went on once Maggie was back on safe ground. "I figured it was his way. But when he was gone…" She breathed deep, consternation marking her gaze. "His fate plagued me. Was he saved? Did he accept God or dismiss him to the very end? I nearly drove myself crazy worrying about it until I realized there was nothing I could do to change the past, but I was plenty strong enough to influence the future of these children. So I moved out of the city, got a job at a thriving medical practice between here and Bozeman and brought the kids out to the country and into church. For the first time in a long time, I feel like I'm totally on the right track, despite our loss. In time, God's love prevails."

Her words piqued Liv. "Didn't you feel betrayed when he died, though? As if God wasn't watching out for you?"

Carrie pondered the question for a moment, then nodded. "I was so sad, then angry, and then depressed and angry again, but I kept praying, hoping I'd understand why things happen the way they do."

"And do you? Understand them?"

Carrie called a second note of caution to Maggie, who seemed to think the top rail was okay to rest on. It wasn't, and Carrie reminded her of that in no uncertain terms. "I think I've learned to separate what God does versus man's free will. That things happen, and we bear the weight of our own choices, but sometimes we're affected by those of others. Family. Friends. People who seek evil. And that made me remember that while I'm not in charge of the world, I'm in charge of my home and my family. It helped me to surround myself with the kind of people I want Brian and Maggie to be when they grow up. Faithful. Strong. Hardworking."

"Like the McGuires."

Carrie smiled quickly. "Yes. And Mick's gentle manner and big old hugs don't hurt anything. He doesn't have to prove himself day after day the way my husband did, although he's every bit as strong and brave. He's just not a crazy risk-taker. I'm okay with that. I'm going to take the kids down to the creek to look for turtles in the sun. They'll be back in school before too long and there won't be time for turtle watching. See ya'."

Carrie's words reminded Liv of herself, only in reverse.

When Jack left her, she'd cocooned herself. She didn't look left or right, and refused to think about dating. And when she finally did start going out again, she sought the total opposite of Jack McGuire. Billy Margulies was a quick-talking sales representative for a pharmaceuticals company, a guy who made his living telling medical staff what they wanted to hear, and blurring the lines of integrity to clinch a sale was in his comfort zone. That should have given her a clue right there.

Jack?

He wasn't a risk-taker the way Carrie described, but he embraced everything with a winner's touch. Baseball. His finance career in Illinois. And now the Double M, growing and thriving under the direction of the McGuire men.

Had she deliberately chosen a man different from Jack to push aside the memories?

When Billy left, he told her he needed a wife whose head wasn't always in books. Did she immerse herself in her work and research in Helena to avoid a deepening relationship with her husband?

No.

Her gut clenched, because the real answer was "maybe." Internal guilt spiked. She'd been a good wife to Billy in many ways, but were they made for each other? Had she taken God's directive into consideration or gone headlong into her marriage thinking she had total control?

With her divorce final, her job gone and doors to opportunity open in multiple directions, how could she pick? How dare she choose? What guarantee was there that she was making the right choice after so many wrong ones?

A soft sigh from the horse reminded her of the task at hand. She hummed softly as she groomed him, letting him adjust to her touch, her voice, while she wondered at Carrie's words.

God's touch versus free will. The two were sometimes at odds, but it had been a long time since she sought the former. Maybe it was time for her own leap of faith.

Her phone buzzed. She set the brush aside and checked the caller.

Jack.

She hesitated, surrounded by the beauty of Jack's life, the ranch, the paddocks, the dry grass meadow. In the distance, three figures grew smaller as they hiked toward the creek, a reminder that life goes on. Hauling in a deep breath, she answered the phone. "Hey."

"Hey, yourself. What have you been doing these past few days? I've called and gotten no answer."

"I answered now."

"True enough. Okay." He paused, then asked, "We've got some things to finalize for the game. Can I stop by tonight?"

Her parents would arrive tomorrow with Grandma and Grandpa, so tonight worked well. "Tonight's good. Around seven?"

"Can we make it seven-thirty? We had a problem upland and Dad and I need to repair some fence, then shift cows and we've only got one extra hand here today. I probably won't get back to the house until close to seven."

"A long day."

"But worth it. And if I get to see you at the end of it, then I'll spend the rest of the afternoon counting my blessings."

Was she a blessing? Had she been a blessing to anyone these past years? Maybe not, but that could change, couldn't it? "I'll make you supper. You come and eat, we'll figure out the last of the concessions and the raffles and we'll be all set for the game. As long as the remaining five guys got back to you."

"They did. All but one are coming. And Garrison can come but he can't play because of contract stipulations to avoid injury."

"We can have him sign autographs, then. He can be a side attraction while you guys are the main event."

His laugh warmed her. "I like how you think. All right, see you tonight. And, Liv?"

"Mmm-hmm?"

"Thanks for coming by every day to take care of the buckskin. He needs a name, but I figure that's your job."

"But he's not my horse." She'd asked for naming rights the day of the auction, but Liv knew the score. If you named an animal, he or she became your responsibility. It was a thought she welcomed and a reality that made her gut-clenching nervous because keeping her distance from Jack was tough. If she let the horse draw her further in? Tough could become downright impossible.

"Near enough. And he deserves a name from someone who truly loves him."

Her heart melted. She'd never been asked to name a horse before, but she'd already christened this guy in her head. "Then he's Little Dill," she told him. "We'll call him Dilly because he reminds us of Dillinger."

"Perfect."

It thrilled her to hear the approval in Jack's voice. "See you tonight, cowboy."

"Until then."

She imagined him touching the brim of his hat, the courtly move destined to win a girl's heart. He'd won hers years ago, and if she was honest with herself, she was in danger of losing it all over again.

Common sense said she should finish the town history and hit the road. She could hole up in a college town and spend her days teaching about old times, former lives.

But the air and the sky and the trees laughed at that option, so she finished caring for the gentle-natured horse and headed back to her parents' house. She'd promised Jack supper.

Was she a good cook?

Not really. But with time on her side and the right recipe, she could pull this together. She'd go home, clean up, head to the Middletons' grocery and get whatever she needed, because this one night she intended to be the best cook she could be.

Right until a midafternoon thunderstorm swept through in an angry fifteen-minute tempest that downed tree branches and a few wires, nipping electricity for over half the town. From that moment on, things went from bad to worse and by the time Jack showed up on her step for his promised meal, she was still airing out the house from her current cooking mishap with a score of Liv–0, old propane cook-stove on the back porch–1.

"Burning supper isn't a big deal. Really. We'll just grab food someplace. Can I come in?" Jack looked over Liv's head to the rooms beyond and pretended to ignore the heavy scent of burned meat and vegetables. "I won't laugh. I promise."

He didn't laugh when he stepped through the front door of the Franklin house.

He sighed.

The gracious old oak dining room table was set for two. Twin candles stood tall in cut-crystal candleholders, and Mrs. Franklin's gold-rimmed china sparkled against an antique crocheted tablecloth, ivoried with age. "Liv, that's beautiful."

"What? The table?" She looked up at him as his meaning dawned and half choked out an answer. "You think I set that for you? Us?"

"Well, it's set for two and looks romantic." Jack stepped past her, swept the table another glance, then drew his attention back to her. "And it is just you and me here. One plus one equals—"

"An old-fashioned dining-table photo op to go with my historical presentation," she cut in. "I'm doing a self-made movie of Jasper Gulch as part of my assignment, so I'm using stills of some things and live shots of others for the slide show component. Jack McGuire, did you really think I spent the afternoon sitting here making a romantic play for you?"

"A guy can hope." He kept his tone light to hide his disappointment, knowing he had no right to jump to a conclusion like that. Although half the town was jumping to their own conclusions once they figured out Liv drove to the Double M daily to care for a horse.

"Just because I burned supper—"

"The evidence of which lingers still." He breathed through his nose and made a face to tease her. "You might want to wash the curtains before the family gets home tomorrow. Or open some more windows. And an extra door or two."

"It's not that bad."

It was, but he wasn't going to waste precious time with her arguing about burned pork chops. And potatoes. And—

"I figured I'd be fine using the old gas burner when the storm knocked the electricity out," Liv continued as she moved toward his truck. "Let me just say, those old propane burners can really torque."

"A lesson learned." He climbed into the truck and nodded toward town. "Wanna head down to Great Gulch Grub?"

"Not on your life," she muttered as she fastened her seat belt with a firmer-than-needed *click!* "Half the folks in town are already buying us wedding presents, it's ridiculous. Lilibeth Shoemaker even suggested we could tie the knot with the rest of the crazies at the Old Tyme Wedding the council dreamed up for October. As if something as sacred as a wedding should be done with fifty couples gathered around a tent. Foolish talk, don't you think?"

The thought of Livvie in a white gown and veil, looking up at him, promising him the forever he jerked out from under her years ago?

The whole thing didn't sound crazy at all; in fact, it sounded pretty darn good, but he'd promised himself to go slow, even though the town seemed determined to go fast. "Let's grab burgers in Ennis, then. I can check out the spot where Coach wants to practice. See if today's thunderstorm did any damage to the field."

"Ennis is good. We won't know a soul in Ennis."

"Liv! Jack! How nice to see you two! Mert, do you see who just came in? It's Liv and Jack!"

Mert's gaze brightened, but she put a calming hand on her aging grandmother's shoulder. "So it is, Granny. Working tonight, folks?"

Mert had given them an out, and for a town gossip whose job gave her proximity to most everything that went on, Mert was going out of her way to cut them some slack. Liv appreciated the gesture. "We're figuring out the last of the details for the Old-timers' Baseball Game, but we lost electric at my house."

"Us, too!" Granny nodded agreement and thumped her cane. "That's why we came over this way, in case they hadn't gotten it back in the Gulch. If half the folks are still without power, Great Gulch Grub will be standing room only and

I wasn't about to mess with that. And Mert's been on her feet all day."

"Well, ours came on just before we left to come here," Liv told the older woman, "so things should be back to normal by the time we all get back home. And, Granny, I had some of your rice pudding the other day. Two helpings, actually." She couldn't help slanting a smile up at Jack. "It was delicious, as always."

"I'm so glad." The old lady sent Liv a precious smile, but then her gaze rosied up as she peeked over Liv's shoulder. "Rusty. Good evening."

"Mert. Clarabelle." The ninety-some-odd voice of wisdom in Jasper Gulch smiled at the two women, then turned toward Jack and Livvie. "We ready for that meetin'?"

Granny's face fell.

Mert's did, too, as if she was really, truly hoping for something long-lasting and good to come out of this reunion story, but she left the topic alone. "We're done, so we'll leave you guys to get the game details sorted out. Have a good night."

"You, too."

Jack tipped his hat, then removed it as they found a seat. Rusty sat with them until the door had long since closed on Mert and her granny, then he stood, and smiled as he started to walk away.

"Rusty. Where you headin' off to?"

"Two's company." The old man waggled two bushy eyebrows in their direction. "We ain't got no meetin', in case you forgot. I'll grab a seat at the counter."

"Come back and sit right here," Liv scolded. "We are having a meeting to finish up details, so it's perfect timing."

"More perfect without an old man around, I'd say."

"Nonsense." Jack stood and pulled out the chair Rusty had vacated. "Sit and eat with us. Let's nail this thing down once and for all. I've got a ranch to run."

"And batting practice, I hear."

"You saw Coach."

Rusty nodded. "Ayuh."

"I figured it was time to grow up. Finally. At long last. Just took me a good while to see things in the right light."

"Well, here's hopin' it don't take you all that long to figure other things out, boy." He sent Livvie an innocent look that made her laugh. "Time's a-wastin' and ain't no tellin' how much the Good Lord's givin'. Which is why I'm ordering dessert for supper tonight. Because at my age, it's not about breaking the rules, it's about which rule to break first."

"Order what you want, it's on me," Jack replied.

"But—" Liv turned his way, knowing she should buy dinner. Her burned food? Her bad, 100 percent.

"Buying dinner is the least I can do when you guys have jumped in to help me get this game organized. Trust me." Jack handed her a menu the quick-stepped hostess dropped off. "It wouldn't be this far along, or this well-put-together if I was doing it on my own. And I can guarantee you it wouldn't be nearly as much fun."

"In that case—" Rusty grabbed up his menu and grinned "—I'm getting two desserts. One for now and one to take home for later."

"Two desserts." Liv made a face at the tall, aging wrangler. "When you're skimming five foot one you have to weigh up the thought of one dessert, much less two. I envy you, Rusty."

"Ach." He reached over and patted her hand. "I've had nearly twenty years alone, Miss Livvie. That's a long time to miss someone, so my advice to you is to live the life God intended and if something comes along to change that? Well, then you can treat yourself to that extra dessert. But right now there's too much life ahead and I'd say it's 'bout time folks grab the reins and hold on for a sweet ride. Because life's not about gettin' there in quick time. It's about the bends in the road."

"'Two roads diverged in a yellow wood…'"

"That Mr. Frost, he was a right smart man," Rusty allowed.

Liv sighed inside. Outward, she smiled. "Well, he's got nothing on you, Rusty."

Her words pleased him. He grinned and she knew their entire town would rue the day when Rustyisms were nothing but a memory, but oh! What a wealth of memories the old sage offered.

"I thank you, Liv. And here's to us and this game." He raised his glass-bottled soda and toasted their small group. "To a great day and a great game, may the Lord be praised."

She clinked bottles with both of them, and realized the burned dinner had offered her a personal road less traveled, a chance to hang out in Ennis with Rusty. With Jack. To see Mert's gentle concern overtake her urge to gossip.

Right now her broken road didn't seem all that difficult after all.

Chapter Eight

Liv stood when Jackson Shaw called out her name the following evening. "Mr. Mayor, councilmen and women—we have a problem."

"How so?" The mayor arched an eyebrow. Others followed suit.

"There are gaps in our town history."

"Gaps?" Councilman Sam Douglas leaned forward. "As in?"

"Holes. Unfilled spots. Places where historical reference to Jasper Gulch may or may not have been deliberately altered."

"Ridiculous." Jackson's doubtful expression said she'd messed up her research. Liv knew that wasn't the case.

"I thought so, too, at first." Liv stressed the time reference. "But when two different modes of research turned up the same empty spaces in time, I realized the likelihood was more than coincidental. So then I delved further."

Was it her imagination or did the mayor squirm in his seat? Of course, the heat and humidity might have been the reason. Still…

"Olivia, where exactly are these gaps?" Rosemary Middleton leaned back in her chair, openly curious.

"The first occurs around the time of the original settlement, when the town is first being established as Beaver Creek Settlement. The name wasn't changed to the present name for nearly fifteen years. In those early years, there is a notable missing chunk about the Massey family—"

"The original cofounding family who came here with the Shaws," Chauncey Hardman reminded everyone.

"Right." Liv smiled over at her. "So there's my first gap, and the second one is around the time of Lucy Shaw's accident."

"Young lady."

Jackson's tone of voice straightened Liv's shoulders and made the hairs along the nape of her neck rise. "Yes, Mr. Shaw?"

The fact that she didn't use the polite "Mr. Mayor" term made Jackson draw himself up taller in his seat. "When an entire town is grieving the loss of one of its most accomplished citizens, the thought of jotting down notes for later reference probably goes by the wayside in favor of prayer."

Liv met his gaze firmly. "In truth, *more* people are likely to journal, jot and reminisce in times of hardship and sorrow, Mr. Shaw. Throughout history, that's when the bulk of our interwoven pasts have been recorded. Few people take the time to record the mundane, but the sensational always has its day. Having said that—" she paused, making eye contact with the group as a whole because she could see Jackson wasn't one bit pleased with her report "—I could use a place to continue my research. I've been using the library, and Robin Frazier has agreed to share her genealogical research study with me if we can work together, but at the moment we're stymied by lack of space and the need to be quiet. My parents' house is no longer an option because my grandparents arrived today from Michigan."

"And our prayers are with your family, Liv," Rosemary cut in. Her sympathetic expression was reflected across the six-member council. Despite some small-town problems, when the going got tough for anyone in Jasper Gulch, folks gathered around to help. "If there's anything we can do, you let us know."

Rosemary's sentiments were echoed throughout the room, and the feeling of warmth that had stolen through Liv the night before reblossomed under the quiet outpouring of support. "We appreciate that more than you know. Grandma is an avid knitter, so if she could join in the knitting group, that would give her a chance to get to know folks." She didn't add that it would also give her grandmother a breather from Grandpa's elder care. The looks of acceptance said most people here understood more than she did about Alzheimer's. "Robin is here." She motioned for Robin to stand beside her. "And if we could have a spot where we could share information, that would be in everyone's best interests."

"We must have a room these gals can use." An upriver cowboy Liv didn't recognize tipped back in his chair a few seats to her left. "Couldn't they use this room during the day? The council only meets on Tuesday nights."

"This room is reserved for possible court dealings," Jackson retorted. "We can't be clearing it of old news and artifacts every time we need to process something or someone."

"The five times a year that happens don't seem like such a big deal to me, but then, I'm a country boy." The rancher met Jackson's glare with a look that said the mayor was being obtuse. Liv couldn't disagree. "But I'm sure that somewhere in this antiquated building there's a spot for these two lovely young ladies to set up shop. You can't hire someone to do a job then expect them to do it on a park bench, Jackson."

Liv drew a breath. No one called the mayor by his first name during a meeting, ever. Jackson ground his teeth, worked his jaw, then shrugged. "You have a point. We'll have something ready for you women tomorrow."

"Thank you."

The entire board looked miffed and puzzled, as if questioning why Jackson had treated the issue in such a gruff manner, but Liv wasn't interested in the politics of the situation. She just wanted a spot to work where she wouldn't be in her parents' or grandparents' way and where she and Robin could share thoughts or ideas for the next few weeks.

As she sat down, her phone buzzed an incoming email from Montana State University accepting her application for employment and wanting to set up an interview ASAP.

Her heart chugged. Her legs turned to stone.

Here was an opportunity she'd been waiting for, a chance to begin a new life, the life of a single professor, living in genteel circumstances along the university boulevards. A few weeks in Jasper Gulch had her rethinking this option completely.

The mayor's demeaning attitude had her fighting mad, so she shelved the email and walked outside with Robin.

"What was that all about?"

"You mean Jackson's attitude?" When Robin nodded, Livvie shrugged. "I have no idea. Jackson's always had a bee in his bonnet over being the best of this, that and the other thing. He's not one of my favorite townspeople, but the Shaw name has gotten him reelected multiple times."

"Money talks."

"Even when it shouldn't," Liv agreed. "But he's got a nice wife who balances things out, for the most part, and his kids are solid. But that—" she hooked a thumb in the direction of the meeting room "—is the reason I limit my dealings with him. And maybe with this whole bridge-reopening drama and disagreement, someone more forward-thinking will win the next election and we'll see changes made."

"You want this changed?" Robin swept the town a look that said she liked things old and rustic. "I think it's charming."

"Charming doesn't give us quick access to medical treatment. Isn't it silly to have only one road that leads toward an interstate? Especially when folks have to travel far for good care? There's nothing too radical about a good transportation system."

"I hadn't thought of that." Robin's expression said it might be worth the trade-off. "Still, I think the warmth and welcome Jasper Gulch offers is worth a little sacrifice. Although fixing the bridge to head south more easily really does make sense. The idea of keeping it closed in memoriam is really kind of strange, isn't it? After all these years? And then putting the new museum on a dead-end road that ends in a broken bridge? I don't get the sense in that at all."

Liv sent a grim look north and shook her head. "Me neither."

"I don't know how a room can smell musty in mid-August, but this one does." Liv pushed open the door to the small, windowless room and waved Robin in the next morning. "Here's where we're working for the duration."

Robin's mouth opened. "It's a closet."

"Yup."

Robin turned toward Liv and her expression deepened. "I'm not being metaphorical. It's really a closet."

"They hauled the maintenance stuff out just this morning, hence the lingering scent of the musty mop bucket." Liv moved to the far end of the narrow space and set up her laptop near an outlet. "Here's my corner. At least we're not far from the library and if we listen close, we can hear the sounds of construction for the new museum."

"We could if there was a window." Robin stared around, then frowned at Liv. "You're really okay with this?"

"Since our options are limited, I'm okay with it for now," Liv answered. "I'm not sure if this is Jackson's own personal reprimand because we asked for space last night or if it's truly the only corner they could find. My guess is the former, but right now I feel like calling his bluff and pretending it's the greatest work spot in the world. Nothing like honey to sweeten the moment, right?"

"Hey." Robin sank into the second chair once she settled her computer at the near corner of the table. "There's a bakery to our left and a café across the street. Color me happy."

"Speaking of which…"

Both girls turned.

Jack strode in carrying a drinks tray with two coffees and a white paper bag. "Coffee and pastries to celebrate your new closet."

"Mock us all you want, cowboy, at least we've got a spot."

"Of a sort." He set down the tray and the bag, crossed his arms, swept the room an amused look and grinned. "I left the coffees black, but your fixin's are alongside. And I've got to pick up a part for Dad's truck and get back to the upper pasture, so I can't stay, but I heard about this while I was grabbing coffee and figured you girls could use a lift."

Robin reached for her cup and sighed. "The closet has just been upgraded to a small French bistro. Well done, Jack. But how'd you know I like coffee?"

"Liv said you two were simpatico. After I looked up what it meant, I figured you must like coffee and old stuff. I understand the coffee addiction." He smiled at Liv and gave her a shoulder nudge with his upper arm. "The ancient history research stuff? That's a mystery to me."

"If we don't learn from the mistakes of the past, we are destined to repeat them."

"George Santayana in slightly butchered fashion," Robin said and laughed.

"Well, I'm leaving you ladies and your history and this George guy to do whatever it is you're doing. Are you taking your grandma to the knitting group tonight?" Jack shifted his gaze down to Liv.

Should her heart speed up like this? Wasn't a racing pulse dangerous to her health? And the rising warmth meant she was blushing. How ridiculous was that, a thirty-year-old woman blushing? She nodded, unwilling to show her nerves by attempting words.

"Good. I'll swing by tonight and treat you and your grandmother to ice cream. I bet she'd like that."

"It'll be late and you have to get up early."

"A little sleep loss is no big deal when you get to take a pretty girl out for a cone. Shame on me if I didn't realize the worth in that trade."

"Okay."

For the life of her, she couldn't put him off, even though that's exactly what she should do. Part of her wished he wouldn't leave, while the other struggled for distance. He put one big, broad hand against her cheek, a fleeting touch but strong. Calming. Masculine. Then he nodded to Robin, turned and went out the door. A light whistle sounded as the distance between them increased, a quick-paced tune that sounded grounded, happy and focused all at once.

Kind of like Jack's father had seemed the week before.

"On a scale of one to ten, one being ho-hum and ten being 'why-isn't-he-on-TV?' gorgeous, your cowboy is a ranking fifteen. And I'm not prone to exaggeration." Robin's expression underscored her words. "The guy is to-die-for good-looking, sweet and willing to sacrifice sleep to see you tonight. If you're not interested, feel free to step aside. I could learn to love ranching like this." She snapped her fingers, laughed at the look Liv shot her, then raised her hands, palms out. "Okay, okay, I get the message. He's off-limits, even if you're not as sure about that as you should be. But what a sweetheart, Liv."

He was a sweetheart now.

Liv recognized that. But was she smitten because it was Jack and old feelings mushroomed whenever he was around? Or did being recently stung by divorce play into this? And was she mentally and emotionally ready to dive into the waters of romance?

No.

Was that normal?

She sure hoped so, because therapy wasn't readily available in Jasper Gulch, Montana.

Church bells interrupted her just then, a warm noise, a reminder of times past.

She'd forgotten that Mountainview rang sweet hymns now and then throughout the day. The quaint custom came back to her as she keyed the City Hall Wi-Fi password into her laptop. She'd grown up hearing that carillon tone in grade school, old songs of praise and patriotism. The sound of home, grace, apple pie and dusty trails.

Her heart stretched open, remembering. As she entered the key words for the familiar research site, her email dinged, reminding her of the message she'd received the night before. The possibility of an assistant professorship, sixty minutes away. Closer than she'd been, but not an easy winter's drive.

She needed a job. She needed a new start. But her mother could use her help right here, in Jasper Gulch. Stay? Go?

How about pray?

She stared at the computer screen, seeing nothing, as the old tune ebbed from the bell tower.

Nothing wrong with praying, is there? You used to pray often. Then you kind of drifted away.

She had drifted. She'd pretty much shrugged off faith and prayer when Jack dumped her. She'd done an abrupt about-face and hadn't given God much of a chance since.

And then she had the nerve to get mad at God all over again when Billy announced his plans for a quick divorce.

God's fault? Or free will and human choice?

She sighed inside, beginning to see that maybe she wasn't innocent in all of this. She'd made choices, too, and maybe her decisions had influenced others.

The chimes softened. Ended. Three sweet notes finished the hymn, *pling...pling...pling.*

Soft and caring, calling folks back to God, if only they recognized the music's plea. She drew a deep breath and made a decision that she would take Grandma and Grandpa to church on Sunday with her parents. No matter what happened, she'd be there, because stubborn rejection was getting her nowhere. Maybe a dose of old-fashioned humility would help. She was pretty sure it couldn't hurt.

Chapter Nine

⟨graphic⟩

"Liv, I'm so glad you came. And this is your grandmother?" Mamie Fidler crossed the foyer of her rustic inn before the wooden entry door swung shut. "Trudy?" Mamie stuck out a hand in welcome. "I'm Mamie Fidler, and over here you've got Carrie Landry and Chauncey Hardman, some of our more ardent knitters. When Carrie's not busy saving lives as a nurse practitioner and Chauncey can sneak away from the library, that is."

The door opened behind them and Mamie smiled over their heads. "And here's Sandy Wilson, who pretty much runs the show out at the Shaw Ranch. Come in, Trudy. Take a seat. Tell us a bit."

Liv's grandmother put out a reluctant hand to accept their welcomes, then sank onto one of the firm, overstuffed, wide-backed chairs that made Mamie's sitting room a comfortable place to gather. Her gaze roamed the room, came to rest on a preserved elk head and the black bear in the room beyond. She breathed deep, obviously unimpressed, and then sighed disapproval. "This is quite the place."

Liv's nerves stretched tight. Grandma wasn't happy about the move Jane and Dave had fairly forced on her, and while she probably appreciated the help with Grandpa Tom, she'd have preferred to stay in her own house, playing by her rules.

That didn't happen and her ill humor over the lack of control was readily apparent.

"Thank you." Mamie sat opposite her, and picked up a gorgeous nubbed ivory shawl. "Has Liv explained what we do here?"

"Just that you guys fill orders for Julie Shaw's virtual store," Liv replied. "I wasn't bitten by the domestic bug that seems to run in my family. My sister Kate got all of that, but she's in Texas, so here I am." She ran a hand over the shawl's edge and met Mamie's gaze. "This is stunning, Mamie."

"I love the classics." Mamie took up her needles and indicated the table of patterns with a dip of her chin. "Trudy, we pretty much do what we're called to do, and then if Julie needs specifics for special orders, we set things aside and jump in. Do you knit and crochet?"

"I do."

"Then feel free to work on your own things or join us in producing items for Julie using Shaw wool. We get paid on a piece scale, but we mostly do it for fun."

"Therapy," Carrie added, laughing as her fingers

nimbly worked through some kind of roundabout stitch as if it was nothing. "No one yells at me here, I'm never accused of being deliberately late and the yarn does what's it's told. Most of the time."

"I was working on this when I had to move."

Grandma's bitter tone stopped everyone's progress as she reached deep into her bag and withdrew a delicate piece. Chauncey recovered first. She set her work aside, moved closer to Trudy and reached a hand of respect to the beautiful rose-toned lace capelet Grandma withdrew from her bag. "Trudy. This is stunning."

"Grandma, it's beautiful."

"Gorgeous." Sandy Wilson nodded from her seat to their right. "And that color would look simply lovely on Miss Julie, wouldn't it?"

"The bride-to-be, yes." Mamie nodded. "It's the right shade for her, Sandy. Trudy, who are you making this for?"

Grandma's face showed indecision. "We had a benefit thing at our old church. Every year I'd make pretties and people would bid on them to raise money."

"That's so nice, Trudy." Sandy leaned closer and warmed the room with her open smile. "Will you send this back to them once it's finished?"

"It's gone."

The women paused, watching her, not understanding. Liv followed suit, because she didn't have a clue what her grandmother meant.

"The church, I mean. Like so much back home, it fell on hard times and they had to shut the doors two years back. I—" She stared down at the intricate cotton piece in her hands, the delicate lace pattern a tribute to old arts. "There is no more benefit, but I couldn't stop myself from making things."

Silence reigned until Chauncey sat forward with a thump. "You kept on, Trudy. When it all fell apart around you, you kept on, and that's just the kind of person we like here in the Gulch."

"There's plenty of truth in that," agreed Sandy. "Trudy, the piece is absolutely timeless and lovely. Would it work in wool, do you think? I'm guessing no because the yarn is thicker. The cotton thread is perfect for that crocheted lace."

"Wool would be too thick and coarse for this one," Grandma agreed, but then she fumbled into her bag one more time. "I thought this old pattern for a fine wool yarn might be nice."

"Nice?" Mamie held up the printed sheet with the half-page picture of a woolen shawl and passed it around. "Trudy, are you comfortable working with needles to produce that kind of lace?"

"So far my hands are good." Trudy raised smooth, straight hands up high. "And my heart and head are working, too. With Tom's situation, it seems good to keep myself busy while keeping an eye on him. Without him knowing, of course."

Empathy blanketed the room. The thought of this aging woman, facing her husband's diagnosis, creating beautiful works of art for a church that no longer existed—Grandma's devotion heightened the gathered awareness.

"Time and change can be friend or foe, our choice," declared Chauncey. "Looks to me like you've chosen to rise above, Miss Trudy, and that's an example we all can follow."

"Yes. Well." Embarrassment flushed Grandma's cheeks, much like Liv's blush that morning. Now she knew where the telltale skin came from. "I can talk and work." She focused her glasses on the end of her nose, picked up her thin crochet hook and started in.

"Liv, if you'd like to come back around nine?" Sandy caught Trudy's eye. "Is that too late, Mrs. Mason?"

"Nine's fine."

"All right." Liv took her cue, stood and moved to the door. "I'll see you ladies later."

"Thanks, Liv."

Mamie called the words as Liv pulled the broad front door open, and when she turned back, Mamie's steadfast expression assured her everything would be fine. Just fine.

Liv wasn't so sure, but they'd made the first step forward, and if she knew Grandma, the old gal would be trying to run the show before too long.

I couldn't stop myself from making things.

Grandma's words painted a picture for Liv, a living room scene of the old couple, alone. Their neighborhood crumbling around them. Chronic change, steady devastation, holed up in their nicely outfitted century-old home while their local world spun out of control. The one constant was Grandma's fancy work, the work of her hands.

"Livvie Franklin? Are you back for good or for a while?"

Liv turned and came face-to-face with Julie Shaw, Jackson's youngest daughter, newly engaged. "For a while at least."

Except, was she? Did Montana State want to offer her a post for the upcoming semester? She'd know next week because that's when they had scheduled an in-person meeting. "How are you, Julie? I hear congratulations are in order."

Julie laughed out loud and grabbed Liv's arm. "Isn't life the strangest thing?"

Cheated on, newly divorced, out of work and sleeping in her childhood bedroom, Liv couldn't disagree. "Beyond words."

"Six weeks ago I was daydreaming about being a wool-spinning spinster, just me and a dog or two, spending my years watching the sheep come and go."

"Julie. That's beyond dreadful. And frighteningly similar to my recent thoughts," Liv admitted as they walked toward Main Street.

"That's the thing, Liv. I forgot who was in charge. Who forges the paths, the bends in the road, and then all of a sudden, there I am, helping out with the rodeo…"

"A target-rich environment," Liv interrupted, laughing.

"I'll say!" Julie laughed with her, but then sighed. "It was like night and day. I caught sight of Ryan, looked into those eyes, and it was like God whispered into my ear, 'He's the one.' Silly, right?"

It wasn't silly at all, because hadn't she felt the same way years before? Heard the same soft whisper of recognition? But it hadn't been about Billy Margulies, the man she married.

The whisper had come about Jack.

Had it been that way all along? That no matter what she felt for Billy initially, he could never be Jack McGuire? Had she undermined her marriage from the beginning because she married the wrong man?

She tamped the thought down and smiled at Julie. "Not silly. Smart. When God and instinct work together, I don't think you can go wrong."

"Well, he'll have to get used to the idea of sheep, and for a cattleman, that allegiance does not come easy. But the idea of sheep and children and ranching and home-cooked meals, once Sandy is able to teach me the ABCs of cooking?" She angled a grin to Livvie. "I think I'll do all right by Ryan."

"I'm certain of it. Are you going crazy, planning the wedding?"

"Nope." Julie shook her head as they neared

Great Gulch Grub. "We're going to get married at the Old Tyme Wedding in October. I figured if my brother is in charge, nothing can go wrong because Cord never messes anything up. And it seems kind of sweet and old-fashioned, doesn't it?" She nodded toward the café and added, "Want coffee or something while we wait? I brought Sandy in because I needed to get some things and she's coming back to the ranch tonight to get an early start on tomorrow. We've got cattle buyers coming in and she wants everything just so for their arrival."

"Sandy's always been like that," Liv agreed, but as they found a seat, she went back to the topic of Julie's wedding. "Julie, tell me what you can possibly think is sweet and old-fashioned about a tent wedding at the fairgrounds?"

They ordered coffee and Julie made a face. "Put that way, it's pretty mundane, but think about those women who came from the East as mail-order brides. Or the big mining rushes that brought so many folks west. They had to wait until a preacher or a circuit judge rode through to get married and they'd all line up together for the ceremony. I think this is the same kind of thing, only we've got a great preacher in Ethan, it's preorganized, which means the event will be nice, and it's a chance to be part of Jasper Gulch history. You figured me for a princess-style wedding, didn't you?"

Liv's expression gave her away, so there was no sense disagreeing. "Absolutely."

Julie's laugh made folks around them smile. "The same thing happened with my sheep farm. People thought I couldn't, wouldn't and shouldn't do it, but I rarely listen to people and just figure God's got my back. Anything else is frosting on the cake."

God had her back.

Julie's simple declaration of faith was more than words. It was intrinsic to her. She'd always had a loving, trusting nature, even when she was a little kid, tagging along with her older brothers' crowd. When they couldn't ditch her, of course. And despite her delicate look, she had a backbone of tempered steel, because running a big animal enterprise wasn't for the faint of heart. "You're amazing, Julie."

Julie waved that off, but her grin widened as she looked beyond Livvie. "Jack, hey. I'm visiting with your girl. How are things at the Double M?"

His girl.

Liv swung about, color pinking her cheeks again, just like it had that morning. For him or because half a dozen folks heard Julie's remark?

Both, most likely. He crossed the room, nodding greetings to people he passed, then surprised Liv by claiming the seat in the booth alongside her, nudging her farther in with his hip. From the way her chin dipped and her color rose, he thought he might want to make a habit of surprising Livvie Franklin. The very thought made him feel better about a long day behind him. "You ladies could take up knitting and then you wouldn't be banished to the diner, you know."

"Or we can recognize our talents lie in other directions and take that road less traveled we talked about."

"Point taken." He slanted a smile up to the young waitress that came by their table, ordered a soda and sat back. "Feels good to perch on something sitting still about now."

"Long day?"

The caring in Liv's question stirred a host of feelings in Jack. He pushed them aside and shrugged. "Bad patch of fence up north. Cows found it. Bad scenario."

"Oh, Jack." Julie's face said she understood. Cattle roaming through fencing often found a tragic end. "I'm sorry."

"Could have been worse and the fence is fixed now, but I feel stupid for not catching it sooner. That ounce of prevention would have been real good in this case."

"Cord ran into that last month," Julie told them. "Said it was because of all the centennial nonsense and sitting on the council and how much was one man supposed to juggle? But I think the real reason was that his engagement fell apart and he just wanted to hit something. So when the far pasture had trouble, he needed something to blame. The town centennial took the direct hit."

"Juggling life and emotion and cattle has its ups and downs," Jack agreed, but as he said it, he realized the old anger he'd harbored for so long had lessened lately. Was it Liv's presence that made the difference?

Maybe.

Thoughts of Ethan's sermon came back to him, how God longs for us to do one thing more. To stretch, to grow, embracing goodness and hard work. He turned toward Liv. "Dilly missed you today."

"I hated to stay away, but I knew Mom and Dad could use my help with Grandma and Grandpa."

"It's going okay?" Jack asked as the waitress dropped off his drink. "They're adjusting?"

Liv shook her head. "Not in the slightest yet, but that will take time. They're like fish out of water right now. Grandpa doesn't recognize anything at our place, so his confusion is deeper. The doctors said that might get better or might not, depending. And Grandma's just plain mad that she had to up and leave her home."

"Liv, I'm so sorry." Julie reached out a hand as she stood. "I've got to run an errand before Sandy's done with the knitting crew, but I want you to know I'll keep all of you in my prayers. I'm sure the adjustment is hard, but I'm going to pray that the reward goes beyond that. And God bless all of you for your willingness to step in and help."

"I don't think there was a choice," Liv told her,

but Julie shook her head and spoke with wisdom well beyond her twenty-four years.

"There's always a choice. Making the right one? That's the tough part. See you guys at the game if I don't see you before."

"Good night, Julie."

"Night."

Folks waved the youngest Shaw off as she moved to the door, and once she'd left, Liv turned toward Jack. "How'd she get to be so smart for being so young?"

"You got me. Ryan's a lucky guy, though. She's a gal who knows her way around a ranch, who doesn't take guff from anyone, and she can wrangle with the best of them."

"A paragon."

Her wry tone made Jack laugh, then he tweaked one of her curls as he faced her more directly. "Jealous, Liv?"

"Don't flatter yourself, cowboy. She's taken, anyway. But the waitress making moon eyes at you from across the room…?"

Jack turned, saw the younger woman staring and flashed a smile back to Livvie. "I guess when you've got it, you've got it."

"*Blech.* Why don't you move over to where Julie was sitting so we don't give folks the wrong idea."

"Not on your life, I think we're giving folks the right idea just as we are. And I'm trusting it's not a one-sided mission on my part."

* * *

Jack, flirting with her. Jack, smiling at her. Reaching for her hand as he teased.

Julie's quiet message came back to her, a whisper on the wind. *He's the one.*

But she'd thought that once and came away brokenhearted and more than a little jaded.

Doesn't matter, scolded the inner voice, sounding a little cross. *What's right is right. He's the one.*

"You okay?" Jack kept his hand resting on top of hers, the strength of big, broad fingers making her feel cherished and safe.

"No. Yes. I don't know."

"Then we take time until you do know." He didn't preface the words with anything, and he didn't belabor the advice, total Jack. Straight-shooting, simple and true. And maybe grown up now?

One look at the stubble darkening his cheeks and chin said yes. Jack was all grown up. And available. And showing an interest she'd dreamed of years ago.

Maybe you never stopped.

That thought humbled her, but as Jack started to talk easily about Dilly and the mares, and how they got through the day, her heart relaxed, listening.

She loved ranch talk. Hearing Julie's tales, reading the tired emotion in Jack's voice, she realized how much she'd missed, living in the city. The air, the sun, the sky, the storms, the daily vivid and vibrant existence of Big Sky country.

She felt good being here. She knew she could help her family if she stayed. But if this job possibility became a reality, how could she turn it down? There was little or nothing to do in Jasper Gulch unless you were a first responder, teacher or rancher. The smattering of shops were capably run with their staff-on-hand, and the local schools weren't in need of additional help.

Which left pretty much nothing in the way of employment for a degreed professional.

"Do you mind if we miss ice cream tonight?"

The tired note in Jack's voice made her want to ease his long day. "Not at all. I'll catch you another time. I'm sure Grandma will be worn-out, and it's probably best to give her time to make the adjustments."

"I'll check in tomorrow." Jack stood, grabbed the check from the young waitress and seemed oblivious to her wide-eyed admiration, a reaction that drew Liv's heart closer to free fall than it should ever be as they left the diner. "You working at City Hall during the day?"

"Not until the afternoon. Mom's got some things to do with Grandma, setting up doctors and all that, so I'm hanging with Grandpa first thing. Then research. Then—"

"How 'bout if you come out to the ranch for supper and we take care of the horses together, then? I'll grill us a steak over the wood fire and we can compare notes on the baseball game."

"The baseball game is completely planned and needs nothing more," she reminded him, but he laughed that off.

"Then we'll just eat and walk and talk. Like we used to, Liv. A long time back."

He paused outside the restaurant door, waiting for her answer, and as an eastbound zephyr played havoc with the left side of her hair, Jack cradled his hand against the errant locks, holding them still. His eyes locked on hers, the scent of his skin a reminder of farm-life jobs and quick soap-and-water cleanups.

Her heart picked up rhythm. Her muscles relaxed. Staring up at him, feeling his hand cupping her cheek, brought a mix of feelings and memories, twined together, indivisible. But for this moment, she didn't want to think rationally. For this moment, she longed to step back in the hourglass and be Jack's girl. His woman. His wife.

"McGuire, you old dog, how's tricks?"

Liv stepped back, saved by an unknown voice.

"Walters." Jack's expression said he rued the interruption, but they were standing in the middle of Main Street, a wake-up call for Liv. Folks would never stop supposing one thing or another when she managed to give them reason to talk by making eyes at Jack in the middle of town. She took a second step back and waved goodbye. "I've got to go get Grandma. Good seeing you, Jack."

"Liv, I—"

"Hey, I didn't mean to interrupt anything," the dark-haired wrangler protested. "Just saw you here and hadn't said hey in a couple of years. Good to see you around, man."

The cowboy's words reminded Liv she wasn't the only hurting soul in this whole scenario. Jack's life had been turned inside out with his mother's passing. He'd stayed secluded until recently. Maybe they both needed time and space to figure things out. She couldn't justify jumping into anything without examining every angle, and that wasn't just the researcher within. That was the woman scorned, twice burned, thrice careful.

Her cell phone buzzed as she approached the inn's entrance. Jack, texting, wondering if she'd agreed to tomorrow night.

She hesitated, eyeing the screen, knowing what she wanted to do and how vastly it differed from what she *needed* to do.

A second text came in, as if he sensed her indecision. She scanned the text then turned to see him watching her from Main Street, his phone held high. She growled at the phone, the few words meant to stir her overt sense of guilt.

The horses, remember? You promised.

He wasn't playing fair, but he was right, so she stabbed a quick yes into the phone with more energy than needed because she knew she should step back. Shy away.

But that was the last thing she wanted to do, and she had promised to help with the horses, a promise she'd break if she moved to Bozeman in two weeks.

The very thought made her restless, but a paycheck was a necessity in the adult world. Having to pay off college loans meant she needed to earn money. But the thought of Jack and the horses and a wood-fired steak?

Those images said Monday evening couldn't come fast enough.

Chapter Ten

❧

"Janie. What's for supper?" Grandpa wondered late the next morning.

"I'm Liv, Grandpa, Janie's younger daughter. Supper's not for a while, but I made tuna for lunch."

Tom Mason peered at her as if sorting her two-part answer was too much. He frowned, glanced around and shrugged. "You got a nice place here."

"Thanks, Grandpa. You haven't seen it in a while."

"What?"

Liv came and sat next to him. Grandpa had been hard of hearing for years, a problem that used to be solved with a pricey but effective hearing aid. Now he wouldn't wear the small earpiece and no amount of cajoling would work, according to her grandmother. "I said you haven't been here for a few years. The last time you and Grandma came to Montana was for my wedding."

"You married?"

She started to answer, but Grandpa beat her to it. "Well, sure you are. You and Dave had a real nice wedding and we threw a great party. The Deans were there, the Garbowskis, the Footes. And the mayor of Deutschtown came. Remember?"

She didn't remember because she hadn't been born yet, but looking into Grandpa's dark eyes, seeing the faded telltale gaze of confusion, she patted his hand and gave him a hug. "What's your favorite lunch, Grandpa?"

"No, thanks, we just had supper. Mom cooked me up some chicken gizzards the way I like 'em."

Mom had done no such thing, and Liv would be amazed to see her mother frying up a cast-iron kettle of chicken gizzards in the kitchen, but if going along was what it took to make Grandpa happy, so be it. "Let me know when you get hungry, Grandpa."

"That tuna sounds okay."

Liv stood up. The worst that could happen would be she'd wrap the tuna and tuck it in the fridge for later. But if she didn't make it and Grandpa decided he wanted it, she'd feel bad making him wait.

He moved to the front porch, sat down in one of the rockers and sighed deep, the slow back-and-forth motion peaceful and restive all at once.

His confusion created a can of worms. He couldn't make decisions, so Grandma made them for him. But he grew angry if he realized he wasn't consulted, so the few moments of clarity became their own problem.

A conundrum of emotion, that's what this illness created. Confusion, mix-ups, misunderstandings, and all because Grandpa's cluttered brain could no longer sift the present from the past with any degree of accuracy.

And Grandma, riled over the move, frustrated by Grandpa's growing restlessness, and upset by a world fraught with change—she'd seemed depressed that morning, and Liv found herself praying for the elderly woman's peace of mind. But when Liv had come back in from putting out the recycling totes, Grandma had been bent over Grandpa, her face serene. "I'm going out for a little bit, Tom. We need to find new doctors here, so Janie and I are taking time to do that this morning. Livvie's here with you."

"Who?"

"Livvie. Your granddaughter."

"You got a granddaughter?" He looked at her, surprised. "Well, you don't look old enough to have a granddaughter, pretty lady."

Her grandma had smiled, patted his hand and stood, but Jane read the fatigue in her face. The stress in her neck, the way she shifted her shoulders to ease the tightening.

But when Grandma turned back to Grandpa, she masked the dismay. He saw nothing but a peaceful smile. "I'll be back soon."

"You bringing your granddaughter along?"

"I just might."

Grandma had turned, saw Liv watching, and she made a face as she came closer. "Half the time I don't know if I should play along or explain the truth. And it really doesn't make much difference because he might not remember either half an hour later."

"But you still try." Liv reached out and hugged her close. "You're pretty amazing, Grandma."

"A body can't quit trying just because things go bad, can they?"

They could. Liv knew that firsthand. But should they? No.

"And I keep thinking if things were reversed, Tom Mason is about the nicest man known to mankind. He'd treat me good if it was my brain having issues. He's been by my side through thick and thin for nearly sixty years. We'll get through this. Though coming here, moving in with your mom and your dad, well." Worry clouded her eyes. "I know it couldn't be helped, but the very thought of starting over made me feel old."

"I'm glad you're here." Liv stepped back and swung the door wide. "I can make up for being stupid and not getting over to Michigan to see you guys more often."

"Oh, Livvie." Grandma made a face that said her granddaughter was being downright silly. "Young people need to live their lives, get settled, get jobs, pay bills. Grandpa and I know how it is, we understand. Don't you fret about things like that."

"I won't now that you're here because I'll get to see you often."

"A silver lining."

Her mother had called Grandma's name right then, and they'd gone off together with plans to have lunch when their errands were complete. That thought sparked interest in Grandma's eyes, and Liv wondered how often she'd been able to get out with Grandpa's condition worsening.

Seldom, if ever, she supposed.

Her cell phone rang with a call from Robin. "Hey, what's up?"

"I accidentally eavesdropped on a conversation in the hall and it seems that folks think the vandalism going on lately is related to the capsule disappearing."

"Except we have no idea why the capsule disappeared, and the rodeo stuff wasn't all that unusual, especially if you've got people who've been partying too much. I don't get how the two things could be linked or why it matters."

"Well, Cal Calloway was here talking to Hannah, and I heard him asking her questions. And he's really nice looking, so I happened to need some water at that very moment."

Liv laughed. "He's a great guy and a good deputy sheriff, but I wonder why he's nosing around

City Hall for answers? But I guess they've got to do some kind of investigation."

"Well, that's just it," Robin told her. The softness of her voice said she didn't want to be overheard. "Mayor Shaw brushed him off, made like the capsule was no big deal and probably a kid's prank, nothing the sheriff's department should worry about."

"He said that? To Cal?" Livvie was no cop, but she'd known Cal since they were kids. Honest, fair and a good ballplayer, Cal wouldn't be put off by the mayor's interference, but he might find his interest piqued. And why wouldn't the mayor want everything possible done to find the capsule and the culprit behind the vandalism at the rodeo?

"He did and the deputy let him have his say, just nodding. Making a couple of notes. But when he left, I got the feeling this wasn't the end of anything."

"For something that's just supposed to be fun, our centennial is taking on a dark side."

"Coincidental, I'm sure." Robin's voice came back to regular level. "And I'll look forward to seeing you later this afternoon, Liv."

Obviously she was within hearing range and attempting to look normal. The thought of Robin Frazier, woman sleuth, made Liv smile, right until she realized she'd lost her grandfather. "Robin, Grandpa's gone. Gotta go!"

* * *

Jack rubbed the tight knot of Liv's right shoulder as she recounted her less-than-stellar elder-care experience.

"I can't believe I lost him."

"You found him." He worked the tight band of muscle stretching from her very pretty neck to her upper arm. "Let's accentuate the positive. Do you knot up like this every time you get tense, Liv?"

She sent a rueful look of affirmation up to him. "From that old riding accident when I was twelve. It tweaked that right side and everything pinches when I get riled up. And no one goes through life without getting riled now and again. But it feels better now. Thank you, Jack."

"My pleasure, ma'am." It was, too, but he held back romantic innuendo because she'd been through a rough experience. "Grandpa walked all the way into town through the back fields?"

"For the first part." Glum, she sighed, and Liv had never been a woman who sighed. "What if something happened to him? What if he'd gone into the creek—"

"It's barely a trickle right now."

"Or wandered into the mountains?"

"He didn't. Quit borrowing trouble and beating yourself up. How'd your grandma react?"

"I didn't tell her."

He pulled back, surprised. "You didn't tell her? Won't she find out?"

"I'm giving it time." Guilt stamped her features. "As much as I need to recover from our little misadventure."

"But someone will rat you out."

"Naw, they won't. When I found him, I pretended he got ahead of me on our walk. Which he did," she added in defense of herself. "Although the walk was an unscheduled part of our morning."

"Wouldn't it help your grandma to know he wandered, though?" Jack wondered. He sat down across from her on the broad front porch and reached for her hands. "That way she can be on guard. I know Cord Shaw gets worried about how Lulu Jensen is getting on. He thinks she's in the beginning stages and she's got a kid to raise, her granddaughter."

"Lulu's about the sweetest, kindest person on the planet."

"I know. It's a problem, for sure. And while no one wants to interfere with her life, there's a twelve-year-old—Cord's goddaughter—who is at risk if Lulu's going downhill. No easy answers, Liv, but maybe if your grandmother was aware of his wanderings—"

"She knows he wanders," Liv interrupted him with a grimace. "I was careless about not closing the front gate. If I had, he might not have slipped out of the yard so easily. But I feel dreadful, locking him in. It's not right, Jack."

"Would you feel that way if it was a kid?"

She looked up, surprised. "To keep a little one out of the road? Of course not."

Jack shrugged. "Same thing, different generation. Your grandpa's reasoning isn't what it used to be. He can't keep himself safe, so it's up to us to do it for him. Just like having a child who can't discern right from wrong yet."

"But it's demeaning. Isn't it?"

"Not in the least. It's respecting this illness for what it is, a rough disease that robs an older generation of reason. But that's where we come in." He stood and pulled her up with him. "We can keep him safe, Liv. You, your parents, Grandma and the town. But only if we look at this realistically and understand his limits."

Tears filled her eyes. For Grandpa? For Grandma? For the whole wretched situation of watching someone you love slowly succumb to a mind-numbing illness?

A mix, most likely, but no matter. He pulled her into his arms, holding her, hugging her, letting her tears wet his shirtfront, wishing he could make this all go away. He couldn't, but he might be able to make things easier by helping out. "Liv, I—"

He drew back and tipped her tear-streaked face up.

His heart melted. His pulse paused, then thrummed as his eyes met hers. The feel of her chin against his fingers, the scent of her hair, sugar and spice, the track of tears slipping down her cheeks.

He didn't ask permission. He didn't want permission, he simply wanted to know if kissing Livvie Franklin would be as perfect as it had been before he messed everything up, and so he dipped his head to find out.

Better, he decided, losing himself in the kiss he'd been missing for far too long. Definitely better.

She should pull back, stop this kiss, apply the brakes to the wave of emotion sweeping over her. She'd come to town with her guard up, force fields firmly in place, but now—*oh, now*—with the feel of Jack's lips on hers, the perfect cradle of his arms supporting her, the cowboy-rancher scent of him, clean and rugged... If there was a scale for kisses, this one...?

Immeasurable.

Her heart rhythm jumped into overdrive. Her head followed suit, not wanting to think or reason, and all because she was kissing Jack McGuire again. Common sense fled the moment his mouth touched hers, and the sensible woman she thought she was disappeared with it. Right now, kissing her former fiancé put her in mind of all things good and right in the world, a feeling she'd love to grasp and hold forever.

A horse neighed from the near paddock. Little Dill, wondering where his nighttime feed was, already becoming a creature of habit.

"Liv."

The moment Jack pulled back, sensibility returned.

"That wasn't supposed to happen," she told him.

"And yet, it did." He planted a soft kiss to her forehead, her cheek. "And I'm not opposed to it happening again, Liv. Like now." He smiled as he glanced from her eyes to her lips and back.

She stepped back and indicated the paddock. "He's calling me."

Jack sighed, rubbed his right hand to the nape of his neck and grabbed her hand in his left. "He's calling us," he corrected her, and the sound of "us" made her heart trip and fall harder. But how could there be an "us" when the mistakes of the past loomed close? How could she trust her heart—and Jack—to consider any kind of commitment?

"You're overthinking things, Liv."

She pulled back and scowled at him. "Nothing wrong with thinking, cowboy. Most of us do it on a regular basis."

He reclasped her hand and tugged her closer as they walked. "Not what I mean and you know it. The minute we stopped kissing, you started putting up mental fence posts and barbed wire."

"My track record says caution is a smart move on my part," she reminded him. "I have an ex-husband who cheated on me for over a year, is now married to that woman and expecting the baby he didn't want to have with me. I'd say I have reason to be cautious, Jack."

"The guy's a fool," Jack muttered. "The thought of having your love and not taking care of it? Listen, take it from a guy who blew that once—Billy Margulies married the most amazing woman in the world and didn't realize it. Having made that mistake myself, Liv? Letting you go because I was a jerk?" He stopped and turned her to face him as Little Dill paced the edge of the near paddock. "It's a lesson I've never forgotten and I'll never make again. And that's a promise I can keep."

Was it?

Looking into his eyes, she read sincerity and warmth. And love?

Yes.

But that look told her more about herself than it did about Jack. It told her that she'd never felt like this, looking at Billy. She'd never had her heart stampede the way it did during that kiss. She'd never—

Realization clutched from within.

She'd been Billy's wife for over three years, and had never enjoyed the wealth of emotions stirred by kissing Jack again.

What kind of woman was she? Had she buried herself in books and work to avoid Billy? Or did she never really, truly love him and married him because she longed for a happy, comfortable ending?

How'd that work out for you? Not so well, I'm thinking.

Little Dill nickered again. She shoved her thoughts aside, knowing there would be time to examine them more closely without tall, lanky Jack McGuire at her side, whistling softly while they nurtured the cast-off horse together.

She'd think about Little Dill and Grandpa, both in need of warmth and affection. If she focused on them, she might be able to see her choices with greater clarity. Stay or go?

Her heart claimed "stay" and declared itself the winner.

Her head?

She filled the water trough, ignoring the flecks of cold water dotting her legs.

Her very logical head reminded her that assistant professorships in history weren't exactly a dime a dozen and if Montana State offered her a contract— which she expected they would because they'd been nudged into a time-crunch situation by a professor's sudden and long-term illness—she'd be foolish to say no. And a single woman with no job didn't have the luxury to be foolish.

Chapter Eleven

"You survived." Coach Randolph made the cryptic comment as he and Jack loaded baseball gear into the back of the coach's van after practice the following night. "No scars, either. Good job."

"I almost didn't come," Jack confessed, and the look on Coach's face said Jack's admission was no big surprise. "Then I realized that if I'm really moving forward, it was time to take charge again. And it was good." He let his gaze wander the Ennis baseball diamond as he tossed a ball into the air. "You've got a couple of nice prospects, Coach." He directed his attention to a group of players nearby.

"Three that stand out, although that Munoz kid could be a dark-horse contender. If we can keep his head in the game."

"And that's tough when you're working two jobs to help your mother make ends meet."

"He does not take kindly to handouts, either."

Jack understood the quiet message. Coach Randolph was in a position to offer help from time to time, but Sonny Munoz wore pride like a cushioned saddle blanket. Jack knew the good and bad points of that, but the kid intrigued him. "He makes it to practice regularly?"

"Always. And then goes to work, catches some sleep and off to school when it's in session. And two little sisters who look up to him."

"And I suspect the ancient car is a daily dilemma."

"Yup. Will it start? Will it make it where they're going?" Coach sighed. "We take simple things for granted. Decent wheels, a roof over our heads, plenty of eats. Kids like Sonny? For them, nothing's a given, everything's a trade-off and time gets short. Real short."

"Like Pete Daniels?" The former Legion ballplayer's tough-guy attitude hadn't served him well on the field or off in his Bobcat-playing days. A talented second baseman, Pete's rude mouth and bad attitude labeled him with the umpires early on, and no amount of coaching changed his attitude. Now, past his prime and angry at the world, the twentysomething minimum-wage worker was always trying to show others up. Pete's sour take on life blemished a God-given talent.

The coach snorted. "No. Pete's never had it easy, but he wants it easy and that's a big difference. His attitude trips him up and I think that's why he never made it into the minors. The baggage he carries made him an unlikely pick. If you're the next

Derek Jeter, a coach might overlook some tough-guy attitude."

"If you're the next Derek Jeter, your coach wouldn't need to," Jack supposed. His words made Coach grin.

"Jeter's one of a kind, a born leader. But Pete, well." Coach rubbed his jaw, then shrugged one shoulder. "You have to want things badly enough to work for them, and if you want them badly enough, it shouldn't seem like work."

Jack believed that, too. If you loved what you were doing, you welcomed the work. He'd done that with baseball. And he'd done that with the ranch. In Chicago, sitting at a desk, orchestrating financial futures?

No.

The realization made him pause as Coach waved goodbye.

He'd done an excellent job for Reiger, Stauff and Mitchellson. He'd hit bonus after bonus, tucking away money at a time when there wasn't a lot of leverage in the markets. But had he loved it?

Not in the least.

He climbed into the truck, but didn't turn the key right away. A light dawned in the back of his somewhat dusty, trail-riding brain.

He worked hard and did well, regardless. And he'd always thought he came home because his mother was ill. She needed him, and this was where he should be.

But he stayed in the aftermath, grieving. Working. Riding herd, mending fence, weaning bawling calves from anxious mothers.

The mental illumination stretched brighter and longer. The lights of the baseball diamond flashed on as a team arrived for a late-day game, but Jack's newfound clarity had nothing to do with the game or the banks of lights.

It was totally about him. He thought he'd stayed out of duty, to help his father, to be a working partner with his mother gone.

A smile softened his jaw. His shoulders relaxed.

Yeah, he'd stayed to help his dad, but mostly he'd stayed because this was where he belonged. Jasper Gulch was more than a little town bent on celebrating its roots. It was an experience to be lived. Loved. Cherished.

Sonny Munoz's face came to mind. A great kid, hardworking, applying muscle to the task at hand. Unlike Pete, Sonny appreciated everything he worked for.

Jack started the truck, cranked the wheel and headed back to the Double M as a seedling of a plan glimmered in his brain. He'd talk to his father, see if they could take on another hand. If they put their heads together, they might be able to make a difference in a young man's life, a kid with great potential. A kid like Jack had been, thirteen years before.

He drove home, ready to take another step forward. He'd survived practice, hadn't looked stupid, didn't cave when he walked into that batter's box to help the elite young athletes with their field workout.

He'd made it through and enjoyed the experience, which made him realize he'd been a jerk for way too long.

But no more.

"Jack. Got a minute?"

Jack was aiming left out of the Jasper Gulch Grocery the next day, but turned right when the mayor's voice hailed him. "I do, but just a minute. I've got to get this cold stuff home. Ice cream doesn't do well in this heat."

"Me neither," the mayor agreed. He pulled out a white hankie and swiped it across his brow. "I'm hoping this hot spell breaks before your big game."

Funny. The words *big game* had taken on a whole new meaning these past few weeks. He'd started out thinking of the Old-timers' Baseball Game in less complimentary terms.

Now? The term *big game* fit the occasion. "Can't change the weather, Mayor. No matter. We'll have fun." He directed his look to the bags containing frozen food, a silent reminder of his limited time. "What can I do for you?"

"I'm a little worried," the mayor confessed, and from the look on Jackson Shaw's face, Jack believed him.

"About?"

"The stuff that's been happening. We don't need trouble around here, we don't need a lot of outsiders coming in and telling us how to do things, and I don't want the rest of our celebration upset in any way. Our centennial has taken months of planning, countless hours of implementation and a lot of resources. We can't take that lightly, Jack."

Jack mused the list. Chauncey Hardman had inspired the hundred-year celebration, the committee had devoted long hours to the planning and success. The mayor, personally?

Jackson Shaw had delegated responsibility and then took the credit himself, but Jack refused to let the mayor's self-centeredness spoil his own growing anticipation for a great day of baseball. "Cal Calloway is playing that day, so we'll have a deputy sheriff on hand. But I've also asked the sheriff's department to send extra patrols around because of the influx of people. And with Hutch Garrison here signing autographs and chatting with folks, we don't want anything to threaten a new Major League Baseball player's career."

Jackson paled. "I hadn't thought about that. What if something happens to him? What if he gets hurt? Can we take that responsibility? Can we afford to take it?" He stressed the financial qualifier and Jack shrugged.

"He's not playing, his MLB contract wouldn't allow that. He's here to greet people and sign his name. He'll be fine. I've also got the volunteer ambulance crew on standby, just in case. If the weather stays hot and humid, a long day in the sun can be as dangerous as a broken bat or foul ball."

"I appreciate how you're taking this seriously." Once again the mayor swiped his brow, but he didn't look as reassured as he should, and that made Jack wonder why. "This is big stuff for Jasper Gulch. Big stuff."

"I hear you." Jack raised the bags in his hand and moved toward the truck. "I'll do what I can, Mayor. Gotta go."

"Of course. Good talking to you."

Jack mulled over the conversation on the drive home.

Was Jackson unduly worried? Maybe not, considering the vandalism at the rodeo. Or was it the disappearance of the settlers' time capsule that had him in a tizzy?

Jackson Shaw was a lot of things, and he wasn't one of Jack's favorite people on the planet by any means, but he wasn't a worrier. So what had him worried now?

"Jack! Jack! Come see what we brought over!"

He climbed out of the truck, grinning. Brian Landry's excitement erased all thoughts of the mayor's angst as the boy bounced up and down. "I'll be right there, bud. Gotta put this stuff on ice."

"Okay!"

When Jack returned to the yard, he tipped his

hat back on his head and whistled. "Brian Landry, whatcha got there?"

"A puppy." Brian breathed the words like the funny little pup was a thing of highest regard, and the expression on the boy's face said he was. "His name's Blue."

"Good name," Jack remarked, hiding a smile.

"It's a real good name for a blue heeler," Brian agreed in a most serious voice. "Your dad talked to my mom and they said I could have him if I keep him here because there's no one at my house to take care of him during the day."

"Did they now?" Jack raised an amused look to his father as he reached out a hand to the mottled-fur pup.

Mick scrubbed a hand to his neck, looking a mite uncomfortable, then he nodded. "Kids and dogs go together. And old Molly could use some company until we get this little boy trained up right to run herd."

"Molly's a cow." Brian peered up at Mick from the ground. "Why does a cow need company?"

"Everybody needs company," Mick told him, and the way he smiled at Carrie when he said it said his father was growing serious about Carrie Landry. Jack glanced her way as she twined her right hand with Mick's left.

"They sure do." She smiled at Mick, and Jack was surprised when his father bent and swept a quick kiss to her mouth.

His father. Falling in love. Two sweet kids, fatherless. A little puppy, just taken from his mother, needing a home. And Livvie, caught between two worlds, wondering what to do. Where to go. Couldn't she see the perfection of this scenario? Staying here, staying with him, building a new life together? He squatted low and reached out both hands. "May I hold him, Bri?"

"Well, sure!"

Here, Jack decided as he stood upright, the pup in his arms. He wanted Liv here, on the Double M, completing the circle of family renewed. Looking at Carrie's and Mick's smiling faces, he knew Liv's journey wasn't easy at present. She'd made that clear.

But if he could get her to stay awhile? Gain more time? Maybe he could convince her to give him the second chance he didn't deserve, but desperately wanted. He played with the pup, whistling as the boy and the little dog followed him around for the next hour. He chatted with Brian about frogs and toads and big hairy spiders building nests over the back light, but he thought about Liv the whole time.

They could build their own house on the slight knoll west of the original house. If they broke ground in the spring, it would be done by late summer, next year.

Three bedrooms…no, *four,* he decided with a grin. Definitely four.

And when he rode out with two ranch hands to

help move cattle to a new range, the picture unfolded before him, a true Big Sky family enterprise. Two homes, extended land, and if old Bo Trimmer decided to sell off some acreage, well—Mick and Jack might be in the market to buy it.

He rode east smiling, alive with plans for a future he never thought he'd have. And it felt good to plan once again.

Liv and Jane opened the doors to the recently dropped-off storage container sitting along the edge of the backyard. The two women squared their shoulders in unison. "Okay, then." Jane faced the wall of goods as she muttered the words.

Liv slung an arm around her mother's shoulders. "It's hard to think of packing an entire life into a storage trailer, isn't it?"

"Extremely hard." Jane's jaw went tight, then she breathed deep. "But so much worse for Grandma and Grandpa, so I'll get a grip and we'll dive into this together."

"Liv?" Dave's voice interrupted the moment. He came out the front door, dressed for work at the highway garage in town, and handed off the phone. "Montana State University for you."

She accepted the phone, aware of her parents' shared look of interest. She stepped away, listening as the human resources representative explained a few things while Liv's heart beat faster with each word.

The rep detailed their potential offer, a good offer, without even meeting her. The official word would come at her face-to-face interview on Monday.

The one-year sub position held the possibility of a tenure-track placement the following year when two professors would be retiring. She'd step in for the professor on extended sick leave and be in a prime position to stay or go. The year of work would pad her bank account and give her a better idea of life in academia. She loved research, but being home showed her the downside of being buried in the annals of history day after day. She liked people. This would give her a chance to help young people explore the value of history.

"We've got a second candidate lined up, Ms. Franklin, and in the interest of time, the department would appreciate your decision when you meet with them on Monday."

"Absolutely," Liv promised. She disconnected the phone and turned. Her parents shared a look before Jane cut to the chase.

"Something you want to tell us, Liv?"

"I think they're offering me a job."

"Which campus?" Dave asked, always quick to nail down facts.

"Bozeman."

"That's only an hour away." Pleased, Jane moved forward to hug her. "That's less than half the distance you were before."

"Yes."

"And drivable on all but the worst days of winter."

True, but—

"Is this job for research, honey? Or teaching?"

"I'd be subbing for a professor going out on sick leave. It's an unexpected opening and they need to fill it quickly."

"Sure, being August and all." Dave reached out to hug her with one arm, but then stepped back and bent lower to meet her gaze. "You love research."

"I do," she admitted. "But I think I've spent the past five years hiding in research. I know that probably sounds stupid—"

Her father jutted his chin toward his wood shop located in the old carriage shed. "I disappear into there regularly. I can empathize."

Jane made a face at him before turning back to Liv. "It's a turnaround, but with nice potential. And maybe it's time to change things up, honey."

"Being divorced, jobless and sleeping in my parents' house would suggest I've already done that, so, yeah." Liv made a wry face. "What's one more major overhaul at this juncture?"

"Except?" Her mother must have read the doubt in her voice, because she paused, studied Liv's gaze, then sighed when understanding dawned. "A part of you would like to stay in Jasper Gulch."

Liv stared in the direction of the Double M and shrugged. "I can't, of course."

"Because?" Her father's expression said one way or another, the decision was in her hands.

"It's too soon to start looking at commitments after I've managed to destroy the most important one of all," she argued. "It can't be right to be even thinking this way. Can it?"

Jane's smile said she wasn't so sure, and Dave raised a hand as he moved toward his pickup truck. "No matter which way you go, honey, it'll sure be nice to have you closer to home."

"Jane? Jane! Can you help me?"

The need in Grandma's voice ended their conversation. The looks on her parents' faces reminded Liv of how much was at stake right now. She shooed her mother into the house and grabbed the first box from the back of the storage container. "I've got all morning. I'll sort out the ones marked Grandma's Room and stack them on the back porch. If I've got time, I'll organize the rest into designated areas so we can tackle the sections one by one. Okay?"

"Thank you." Jane gave her a brief hug and hurried inside. The ensuing quiet gave Liv time to think.

Too much time.

Because when she had time to think, the only thing she could think about was that kiss. Jack's scent, the feel of her head against his chest, his arms holding her. His cowboy look, the lazy smile, the quick grin.

She'd fallen in love with him all over again, then

realized she'd never stopped loving him the minute his mouth met hers. What kind of woman did that make her?

Awareness threatened from inside.

She'd taken the scholarship for her advanced degree in Chicago out of spite when Jack broke up with her. She'd wanted to prove how strong she was, that she could be in the very same city as Jack McGuire and not crumble or beg for his attention. And she'd done it, too.

Then she'd gone stubbornly on, developing a life with Billy under false pretenses. She'd gone into a sacred commitment with a singular focus and industry, not unlike her current job quest.

Regret speared her.

Was she shallow? She hadn't thought so; in fact, if someone had approached her eighteen months ago and asked if she was happy, she'd have said yes.

She'd have been wrong. She knew that now. And while there was no excuse for Billy's philandering, she had a better view of the big picture of their marriage in retrospect. She'd used him to get over Jack McGuire, but she'd never really gotten over Jack, so who bore the deeper sin? Her sin of omission? Or Billy's more obvious transgressions?

Her cell phone buzzed a text from Jack. Church, Sunday? Then breakfast together?

She stared at the message, conflicted. If she was going to teach in Bozeman, she'd be close enough to come home on a more regular basis. That could give her time to reexamine these feelings for Jack.

Reexamine? I think that kiss was a pretty good indicator, honey. Unless you're anxious to reexamine the kissing part. That I'd understand.

She shushed the internal reminder as she considered his invitation. Being seen in church would deepen the already invasive speculation in Jasper Gulch. Then going to breakfast afterward?

Sharing Sunday-morning pancakes at Great Gulch Grub was better than a marriage proposal in these parts.

But refusing Jack's invite held no appeal whatsoever, and her examination of conscience said she had some thinking to do. And maybe praying, too.

The toll of the recorded morning carillon interrupted her thoughts. Her parents' home was at the outside edge of town but close enough for the musical reminder of God, first. She'd forgotten that.

Not forgotten. Shoved aside. Let's start this whole new thing with some honesty, okay?

Honesty it was. She texted back Yes, what time? and when her phone rang almost instantly, she knew she'd made the right decision. The ramped-up beat of her heart offered its own evidence as she accepted the call. "Hey, cowboy."

"Be ready at eight forty-five, okay? We'll catch the nine o'clock service. The late-day one is too crowded."

"Silly people, wanting to sleep in on Sunday,"

she teased, but then smiled inside. An early Sunday morning with Jack sounded perfect, despite her misgivings. "I'll see you then."

"We've got buyers coming in from New Mexico," Jack went on. "Otherwise, I'd ride in tonight and go over game details."

"I think we've gone over every detail imaginable already."

"Which would leave us plenty of time to sort out other things." He sounded quite happy to sort out other things with her, and the note in his voice made her insides uncoil a little more.

"You and I having too much time on our hands could lead to trouble."

"Aw, Liv." The smile in his voice told her exactly where he was headed, cowboy through and through. "Shucks, ma'am, kissing you ain't one bit of trouble. Not for this cowhand."

She could play along or ignore his teasing. Either way, she was in a fix, because being near Jack just made her long to be near Jack more often, but shouldn't she know her own mind, heart and soul first? "I'll be out to take care of Dilly and the mares tomorrow. You'll probably be showing the cattle by the time I get there."

"Carrie and the kids will be here. She's making us dinner, and the kids are going to work on a summer project. Brian's got a surprise to show you."

Her heart mushed at the thought of the serious little boy keeping a secret, sharing a surprise.

Thinking of what Carrie's family lost made her realize how precious life and love truly were. Neither should be meted out in neat terms. They should be embraced. Celebrated. Enjoyed. "I can't wait. Gotta go. I'm helping Mom with the storage unit, then Robin and I have a date with our musty closet converted to an office."

His laugh made her feel better about most everything. "I'll see you Sunday, Liv. But honestly? I'll miss you from now till then."

He hung up before she could say another word, and what would she say? What could she say?

That she missed him just as much? That her heart yearned to see his name in her phone readout and hear his laugh?

Being here with Jack felt right, but could she trust her instincts on life and love? She'd been wrong before, and if she and Jack messed this up, it wouldn't be a quiet wrongdoing, not in a town this size. Everyone would know, gossip, share, take sides.

You never worried about such things before and you shouldn't worry about them now. Worry isn't of God, it's of fear. Buck up. Life and love aren't for wimps. Straighten that backbone, girl.

That's exactly what she needed to do.

She hauled the marked boxes to the back porch, setting them just outside the kitchen door. By the time she was done, the boxes slated for the house were neatly stacked, and the storage unit was organized into four accessible sections. The pod was rented for a month, and could go longer if needed. But a month should give them enough time to sort through the seventy-four years of her grandparents' lives. And while that seemed sad, it made her feel helpful. And she hadn't felt like that in too long a time. Her fault, she knew. But now she had a chance to make things right and she intended to take it, one way or another.

By the time she met Robin in their mutual closet, the afternoon was half gone. "Sorry I'm late. I didn't think sorting the trailer pod would take so long."

Robin pointed to a six-pack cooler filled with iced teas. "I figured this would be a nice break from coffee because it's beyond stifling in this room. And I brought that." She pointed to a small fan, busily puffing air around the cramped, four-walled space. "If nothing else, it gives me a false sense of control."

Liv started to laugh but stopped when Abigail Rose called her name. The Centennial Committee secretary was accompanied by Jackson Shaw. Would the mayor notice they were dripping with sweat in the confines of the janitor's closet? Would he care?

Most likely not. She planted a serene look on her face as she turned. "Hot one today, isn't it?"

Abigail held out her hands with a quick glance down. "I always do cool shades of pink for the dog days of August. Although this shade might be considered warm. What do you think, Liv?" She fluttered her hands to draw attention to the current shade of polish. "No, don't even bother answering. I can see it's too warm, much too warm! I'll change it up later."

Before Liv could digest Abigail's spiel, Robin stepped forward. "Can we help you guys with something?"

"The mayor and I wanted to talk to you girls privately," replied Abigail in a voice that defied any vestige of privacy in the old-time City Hall. She leaned close, her gesture inviting secrecy. "Have you found out anything concerning L.S.?"

The mayor swiped a hand to his head as the heat of the room hit him. "Really, Abigail Rose—"

Abigail slid her glasses down, scorched him with a look, one of the few people in town capable of doing that. She then shifted her attention to Robin and Liv. "Of course, the note could be a red herring. That's a—"

"A planted clue to throw us off track," Liv interrupted, hoping all her years of education weren't completely wasted. "Or it's…"

"A bona fide clue." Abigail didn't try to hide her excitement because crime and vandalism didn't go hand in hand in their hometown. "And if it is, you girls might have the answer."

"But we don't." Liv wished she had something solid to tell them, good old concrete facts, but the lack of notation about the time capsule in the historical records was notable. If a town went to the trouble to bury a capsule all those years ago, wouldn't someone, somewhere, have listed the contents? Not in any records they found, unfortunately, but that only made husband-hunting Lilibeth a less likely suspect in Liv's opinion.

"What was in that capsule?" Abigail went on. "Why would someone dig it up? Was it simply an act of vandalism or was there something of value buried there all these years?"

The mayor swiped his sleeve to his forehead, clearly hot and irritated. "What could there possibly be? This is ridiculous, Abigail. The culprit's clearly someone trying to stir up trouble. Anonymous notes, stolen capsules—"

"Arson."

The mayor gulped at Liv's taut reminder, and something in his gaze said he shared her concerns…and maybe others, as well. His expression darkened, then eased as Robin supported Livvie's assertion.

"If there was something of value, we sure haven't found a glimmer of it," Robin assured them. "The few mentions we've found have been somewhat stuffy announcements of period items. Clothing. First newspaper. Letters from soldiers during the First World War. So while they have historical significance, we didn't find evidence indicating anything of substantial worth."

The mayor's sigh drew Liv's attention. He looked almost happy that they'd found nothing of greater import, but that did make sense in a way. Better a simple act of foolish vandalism than a crime of greater magnitude. "And FYI—we've also found absolutely nothing that ties Lilibeth to the capsule in any way, shape or form. The very thought of suspecting her is ludicrous." Liv met Jackson's narrowed gaze with one of her own, daring him to challenge her.

He didn't.

"She was very angry when she didn't win the crown of Miss Jasper Gulch. And that kind of misplaced anger..." Abigail's expression suggested that scorned beauty-pageant contestants were capable of most anything.

"Her initials match." The mayor kept it simple. "And she's a scatterbrain for sure, always fussing with that blond hair, tossing it about."

"Being blonde doesn't make one a scatterbrain," Liv reminded him with a cool look. "She's young, impetuous and a little spoiled. Last time I looked, none of those were criminal offenses, and I can't believe she'd have anything to do with dirt, digging or a shovel. You guys are barking up the wrong tree on this one. Robin?" She turned to face Robin more directly. "What do you think?"

Robin's hesitation said she struggled with both sides of the argument. "Normally, I'd agree, Liv, but Lilibeth does have a temper. And her initials match."

"I'm guessing we have a bunch of folks in town with the initials L.S.," Liv countered. She turned back to Abigail and the mayor. "We'll keep her in mind as we work, but I can't put any credence in the suspicion. And if Cal Calloway and the sheriff's department haven't found anything tying her to the incident, I'm surprised you're still pursuing it."

"That's an excellent point, Liv." Abigail's expression said she agreed with Liv's belief in the local county sheriff's office. "If you do turn up anything that might offer the committee more insight, you be sure to let us know. Okay?"

Liv put a reassuring hand on Abigail's arm. "We will. And, Abigail, honestly? I love that shade of pink for August. I don't think it's too warm at all. It matches the coneflowers in my mother's garden."

Abigail's face lit up. "Does it, now?"

"Yes. And if it works in Mother Nature, why not in the nail salon?"

"You're absolutely right, Olivia! I'll leave it for the day. There's always a new shade tomorrow, right?"

"Absolutely."

The mayor moved off, not bothering with pleasantries like simple goodbyes. Abigail hurried back upstairs, pleased that her polish could stay, although it wouldn't surprise Liv to see the older woman come down later with a new shade, regardless. Abigail's frequently changing nails were the talk of the town and she liked it that way.

When Liv turned toward Robin, a hint of sadness struck her. "Robin. You okay?"

"Fine." She frowned, then shrugged. "It's just they've got very little to go on and they're more than willing to assume Lilibeth must be the culprit based on a note that might be fraudulent. I liked it better when I thought everyone in town was sweet and nice and sang 'Kumbaya' at campfires."

Robin's lament painted an image that made Livvie laugh. "Welcome to small towns. And I agree, I think they're wrong and I hope they don't come up with some kind of harebrained crusade to catch Lilibeth, because the only thing that girl is guilty of is being young and boy-crazy. There isn't a criminal bone in her body and I'd stake my researcher's credentials on it. And on that note." She grabbed a cold bottle of iced tea and pressed it against her cheeks before twisting the cap off. "I'm going to pretend it's ten degrees cooler here and get to work."

"I'll join you."

By the time they closed things up a couple of hours later, Liv was even more convinced that Lilibeth wasn't involved in anything more sinister than boy-watching and big hair. And if the committee thought otherwise?

They would be proven wrong.

Chapter Twelve

"Grandpa? Wanna take a ride with me?" Liv proposed the idea early the next morning, but purposely hadn't run it by Grandma first. Grandma's nerves would likely prompt her to say a quick no. Liv wanted a chance for Grandpa to say yes. "I'm going out to a friend's ranch to take care of some horses and it's a beautiful day."

"You got some horses?" Tom perked up and glanced around the living room as if expecting a stampede. "Where are they?"

"My friend Jack has some horses," she explained patiently. "He lives on a ranch outside of town and I told him I'd come and work with the horses this morning. Wanna come along?"

"Liv, I don't know." Grandma moved into the room quickly, her face creased in worry. "If you're busy, he could wander off. Get lost. And those ranches are a ways out with lots of brush country."

"I like horses." Grandpa planted his two feet

firmly on the ground and stood. "Always did. Yes, I want to go. Trudy, where's my hat?"

"Here, but I don't think this is a good idea," she protested. She wrung one hand with the other. "How about if I come, too?"

"I don't need watchin', old woman."

"Well, you're wrong about that, you old coot," Trudy retorted, but she gave him a good-natured peck on the cheek. "I might just like seeing these horses, too, did you think of that?"

Grandpa huffed toward the car, muttering a mile a minute, and when he was far enough off, Grandma turned to Liv. "I know you mean well, honey—"

"But you're worried I might lose Grandpa or set him up for disappointment."

"Well, I heard about his little jaunt last week," Grandma explained as she grabbed a thin, cotton sweater in case it got cold. The morning temps were in the seventies with no cold front in sight, but Liv understood Grandma's defenses. Be prepared and do what proved necessary. Those two credos had done well for the older woman so far. "And while that turned out okay, he's a handful sometimes, Liv. He's usually nice and mild-mannered, but every now and again he gets plain mad and mean-tempered. And that's what worries me, because I can't say when it might happen."

"Then we double-team him," Liv decided. "We do the 'shift.'"

Her grandmother drew a blank at the baseball term.

"It means we shift strategies to make sure we're one step ahead of him, working together."

"That could work," Trudy declared. She climbed into the backseat and rode quietly until they got to the Double M. When Liv turned down the long, winding lane that led to the homestead area, she saw her grandfather's eyes widen and her grandmother's hands clasp. "Liv, this is lovely. Kind of rustic and country-and-western, and oh, my stars, Liv! Do you see those cattle coming this way?"

"I do."

"Tom?"

"I'm not blind, Mother, just a little daft as the years go on. They're quite a sight, aren't they? And real, live cowboys to boot."

"Beautiful." Trudy climbed out when Liv parked the car. She reached to help Grandpa out, but he'd already undone his seat belt and opened the door. He stepped out, sure-footed, as if there wasn't a thing wrong with him, his gaze upturned, watching the cattle drive, framed by two bushy eyebrows raised in appreciation.

"They'll be bringin' them down to the far corral," a voice said from behind them.

Liv turned and saw Rusty leaning on a fence rail. "They decided to show them down here?"

"Easier to load 'em here." Rusty raised his gaze to the upper lands and then shrugged away from the split-rail fencing. "I'm Rusty, a friend of the family."

"Whose family?" Trudy turned his way and held out her hand. "I'm Liv's grandmother and this is her grandpa. We've just moved into town."

"I heard tell, ma'am, and I also have it on good authority that you make one of the meanest apple pies around. And that we need to get in real apples from the Great Lakes to have things taste right."

Grandma blushed, hearing her words come back to her.

Grandpa turned, sent Rusty a grin and a nod, but then swung back to watch the spectacle of cattle, waving en masse, a fluid curve of movement, working their way down the dry slope. "They kick up a lot of dust, don't they?"

Rusty smiled at Grandma to show he was teasing, then nudged his hat back while he moved to Grandpa's side. "This time of year they do. And when the wet comes barrelin' down from up north, it's greasy slick to bring them up and down. But Jack and Mick, they've been doin' this awhile. They're good."

"Jack?" Grandma moved closer to Liv and kept her voice low. "Isn't that the name of the young man you went with before? The young man you were engaged to in college?"

"Yes."

"Well." Grandma pondered the sight and Liv's admission, then turned toward the corral behind them. "You said there were horses?"

"A fair number, but the ones we're caring for are on this side of the frontmost barn." Liv started to lead the way, then turned back to call Grandpa's attention. His face was outturned, watching the progression of horse and cattle. Rusty gave her a smile and a nod, a look that said he understood what couldn't be said, and he'd watch after Grandpa while they moved off.

A gentle heart and a keen mind, even well into his nineties, the old rancher had seen a lot of Jasper Gulch history. If she really wanted to know things about Jasper Gulch, she should sit down with Rusty Zidek and get it straight from the old gentleman's mouth. And better sooner than later in light of his age. She couldn't take his testimony as absolute fact without some corroboration, but if he steered her in the right direction, he'd make finishing her job in Jasper Gulch easier. And regardless of what decision she gave the university, she was determined to get the town history done before the end of the year. If she took the teaching position, she'd travel back on weekends as weather allowed, and finish her report that way. It wasn't an ideal plan, but it wasn't all that bad either, because weekends in Jasper Gulch meant seeing Jack…

And that thought made her smile like a schoolgirl, so when she called Dilly's name a little too loud, the healing horse jumped, startled.

"Is he wild?" Grandma asked, stepping back. "Liv, you didn't tell me he was wild, for pity's sake!"

"He's not," Liv whispered. She moved closer, tapped softly on the rail and waited patiently as the buckskin eyed her. "Come on, old boy, I didn't mean to startle you, but you've got to get used to a bit of noise now and again, don't you? But there now, that's enough for the moment, come over here and show Grandma what a sweet thing you are."

The buckskin hesitated, eyes wide, then peeked around Liv, watching Grandma. He must have decided the older woman wasn't any too dangerous because he padded forward, head down, waiting for a scratch behind the ears.

"Good boy." Liv reached out and gave him a good scratching where he liked it most, along the back of his neck to the left of the mane. "You're such a love, Dilly."

"He's kind of mangy looking, isn't he?" Trudy moved closer. Her expression said she'd love to compliment the big horse but honesty prevailed. "What's wrong with him?"

"Neglected, abused, uncared for." When Grandma's mouth dropped open, Liv faced her and nodded. "We saw him at auction. Another rancher was going to rescue him, but he reminded me of the old horse I rode here when I was young, so Jack and I brought him home."

"Home."

Liv heard more in the single word than her grandmother should know, but Trudy Mason had a lot of experience in her seven decades. "Here, I mean." Liv waved around the ranch as she moved to the barn to get the horse feed. "To the Double M."

"Mmm-hmm." Her grandmother's tone said she read the situation with solid accuracy, and that made Liv realize Grandma wasn't alone, most likely. It was almost as if the town had planned this centennial celebration with one goal in mind, to bring her and Jack back together.

"You know, I've watched many a thing go on in my life," Grandma whispered as Liv brought food to Dilly in the near paddock. "The Lord giveth and the Lord taketh and things that bore no reason I could see. But sometimes, honey, the path the Lord gives us is so plain and simple as to be too easy. And there's many a person who misses it because of that. Thinking, questioning, weighing things up. Sometimes we have to go with our gut, with our heart."

"You're too smart, Grandma."

"Not by half, but I'm old enough and experienced enough to know if God gives us a second chance in this life, he expects us to grab hold and take it.

And I think that's what's going on with you and your Jack."

"He's not my Jack, Grandma." Liv let a note of caution creep into her tone, all the while wishing he *was* her Jack, and that made her feel foolish.

"I expect you're wrong about that," Grandma continued, her voice soft. "But either way, it's good to take the reins God gives us and ride with them. I'm all right with the road less traveled for a time, but there's a reason folks opt for a well-trod path in life. Because it's the best way to travel."

Wise words from a smart woman.

The noise of the heifer drive grew behind them. Shouts of encouragement, yips of dog and the bawling of first-time pregnant cattle meant the chosen cows were nearing their destination.

"Livvie! Come see over here!" Brian's voice hailed her from the foreside of the adjacent barn.

"You won't believe it!" Maggie's excitement added to the moment, her glee-filled voice spiking upward.

Liv gave Dilly another long stroke of her hand, then walked around the far edge of the next barn. When she made the turn to the left, she laughed and dropped straight to her knees. "Brian! Maggie! It's a puppy!"

"Yes!" Maggie screeched the word, then clapped two sturdy hands over her mouth when Carrie's look reprimanded her silently. "I forgot to be quiet again, Mommy! I'm sorry!"

"Try harder," Carrie advised.

Brian braced two confident arms around the funny pup and lifted him into Liv's lap. "Isn't he the most beautiful thing ever, Liv?"

He wasn't. From the tip of his black nose to the end of his mottled tail, the little heeler looked like a scrambled mismatch of dog colors and shapes, but the bright look in his eyes and the quick-wagging tail won her heart, regardless. "Oh, he is, Brian. What's his name?"

"Blue."

"Well, of course." Blue was the perfect name for this little fellow, a dog destined to learn the ropes of rustling cattle and chasing frogs. "When did you get him?"

"A few days ago," Maggie told her. She crept forward, trying to follow her big brother's example of calm and quiet, but those adjectives seemed alien to the girl's vibrant personality. "Isn't he so sweet?"

He was, Liv decided. She sat in the dirt, the little pup looking for a comfortable position to snug himself in, reminding her of too much. Long days with Jack and his parents, working the ranch. Training horses, training dogs, mixing up cakes and cookies with Mary Beth when chores were done.

And Tank, her big, blond Labrador retriever, a trusty friend gone while she lived a couple of hours away, rarely visiting.

The scent of dog, dust and dreams overwhelmed her. This felt like home. This had been her destiny all along. To be here, beneath the broad, blue Montana sky, surrounded by mountains and wonderful people, one with the land. Why had she ever thought otherwise?

"Liv? You okay?" Brian bent and peered up at her. Worry creased his brow. "Do you want me to take him?"

"No, no. He's fine. I'm just being silly because he reminds me of when I used to hold my old dog."

"You had a dog?" Maggie crept in alongside and reached out a hand to the motley pup. "What was his name?"

"Tank."

"That's a funny name!" Chagrined, Maggie slapped her hand over her mouth, sent a guilty-as-charged look to her mother, then continued in a softer tone. "Why did you name him Tank?"

"He was the biggest puppy of the litter, with the biggest appetite of all, and when he moved, he moved slow."

"Like a tank," Brian mused.

"Exactly." Liv rewarded him with a watery smile. "And as he got bigger, he grew into his name. Big. Broad. Busy. A tank, through and through."

"You miss him."

She hadn't realized how much until Brian tucked the little pup into her lap. She'd accepted Tank's passing as one more regret, coming home, but why hadn't she come back sooner? Hung out with the aging dog, the friend of her youth? Was she that selfish? That self-focused?

Shame coursed through her, but Grandma bent alongside to pet the tiny dog. "I've always been shy of pets," she told Brian. When he looked confused, she lifted both shoulders in a matter-of-fact motion. "They don't live as long as folks do, and I've always been a little afraid of losing things."

The boy's eyes widened.

"But now I look back at my life, and I wish I hadn't been afraid," Grandma continued. "Think of all the puppies I might have raised. The dogs I might have loved. The walks I missed because I was too afraid to get attached."

"Grandma, I—"

Grandma waved off Liv's commiseration as she straightened. "Ach, it is what it is, Liv, plain and simple, but if I had it to do over again?" She smiled down at Brian and laid her aging hand atop his head. "I'd have had me some cute pups like this. Probably more than one because a dog's love is a beautiful thing."

The clip-clop of a horse drew their attention. Jack and Roy-O appeared. Jack's expression said the sight of them made him happy. Right until he spotted Liv's face. "Liv, you okay? Hey. What's wrong?" He was off the horse and by her side in a flash. Concern painted his dirt-streaked features, and the sight of him, dust-covered and worried about her, nearly did her in.

"I'm fine, I just got all choked up about the puppy and Tank and remembering. Silly girl stuff."

"Not so silly." He said the words softly as he reached in to pet the pup. The baby dog sighed, whimpered, then sighed again, blissful in sleep despite the gathered attention. Seeing Jack's big, broad hand gently stroke the tiny puppy made her wonder what he'd be like with children...

Their children.

Tiny babies, then precocious toddlers, running amok, racing after puppies and dogs and cattle. Naughty little boys and sassy little girls, pigtails flying as they learned to ride herd alongside their daddy.

Heat blazed her cheeks.

She was wading into dangerous territory, day by day, moment by moment, knowing she should back away, and helpless to do so.

"I've got to get back and help load the heifers. Will you be here later?"

She shook her head, not ready to trust her voice to words.

"We've got to get Grandpa home," Trudy explained, and Jack stood, smiled, swiped his hand to dirt-streaked jeans and extended it to Grandma.

"I'm Jack McGuire, Mrs. Mason. Welcome to Montana."

Grandma took the hand and didn't raise a fuss about cleanliness. "This place is something, Jack McGuire. Really something."

"It is." Carrie smiled across the kids. "Brian and Maggie come alive whenever we're here. It's as if they've come home."

Liv exchanged looks with Brian. His quiet gaze agreed with his mother's assessment. He was home, here on the Double M, even though horses made him nervous and crowds of cattle gave him reason to walk the other way. Something about the ranch…and the ranchers…embraced the lonely traveler within.

"Liv, gotta go. I'll call you later."

"Okay."

She longed to say more, much more. To tell Jack how the combination of puppy, little kid and neglected horse rolled into her heart, but all that would have to wait, and a good thing, too. Otherwise, she'd be throwing herself at Jack McGuire, and that might not be the brightest choice of the day.

He tipped his hat, remounted Roy-O, turned and rode to the far paddock, the sight of man and horse a rhythmic Western poem. She loved him. She knew it, heart and soul, and probably had never stopped loving him.

Her bad, for thinking she was in control. But now, what should she do? Which direction should she take? Opt for safe and take her own sweet time at age thirty? Or throw caution to the wind?

Is a little time such a bad thing? Getting your bearings, feeling your way?

No, but a full-year commitment to the university wasn't a little time. Not when she'd cast eight years aside already. Why wait? Why hesitate?

Are you forgetting the broken heart he handed out the last time you got serious? And the one that followed your last romantic choice? Are you kidding me?

Indecision plagued her, but as she and Grandma walked back to Dilly and Grandpa, the warmth and scents of the ranch swept her. She'd promised to attend the morning service with Jack, a leap of faith in many ways. But what would she find in the quaint, historic church? Better yet, what was she looking for?

Liv wasn't at all sure how to answer either question.

"Liv, you're going with us." Jane angled a look of surprised approval as Liv entered the kitchen early the following morning. "I'm so glad. Are you bringing your car or do you want to ride in the backseat with Grandma and me?" She fiddled with the timer controls on a Crock-Pot of chicken-and-potato stew, then peered at Liv over the glasses that had slipped well down her nose.

"Jack's coming by for me."

"Really?"

"He is?" Dave came into the kitchen from the back door, and the look he sent her—an expression that wondered if she knew what she was doing—

spoke more than words. "That'll add fuel to the tongue-waggin' fire."

"It's not a marriage proposal, it's a Sunday service. I wanted to meet the new pastor before next weekend's game."

"Hey, if it gets you back in a pew, I'm not about to question the reason." Dave laughed, chucked her right shoulder with a playful nudge, then peered up the stairs. "No Grandpa yet?"

"Not a peep."

"Well, I'll—"

"Dave? Can you help me with Grandpa?" Grandma's voice put a quick stop to their discussion.

Dave winked at Liv and moved up the stairs at a quick clip. "Coming."

By the time they got Grandpa convinced that it was Sunday and he needed to get dressed, Jack had pulled up the driveway.

Liv's hair was a mess of curls from going to sleep with it wet, she hadn't had time to even think about makeup and her white sandals were smudged with ranch residue, leaving her nothing but sling-back heels to wear, which meant a skirt. And a summer top. And a clip to pull her locks back, away from her face.

"You're absolutely beautiful, Liv." Jack stopped and stared, a look of pure male appreciation lighting his eyes. He extended an arm and led her to the pickup truck. "Not like that's a surprise or anything."

"Beautiful. Right." She climbed in, made a face at him and ticked off her fingers. "I barely had time to brush my hair, much less do something with it."

His glance to her hair said he liked it just fine as it was, long and tumbling in its own form of disarray.

"No makeup. My nails are a mess. And my sandals were dirty so I had to wear heels."

Jack looked down, surveyed the shoes and grinned. A light, short whistle said he didn't mind the sassy shoes, either.

"It's all well and good for you," she scolded as he climbed into the driver's seat with barely enough time to make it to town, park and get into the old-fashioned church at the opposite end of town. "But five people with one bathroom makes for a tight morning when we're all trying to get out of the house by eight forty-five."

"Your grandparents are coming?"

"Yes. Grandma's kind of excited, Grandpa was prickly as a trapped mountain bear because he didn't believe it was Sunday and then couldn't imagine why anyone would be going to church this early."

"A lot of changes, Liv." Empathy softened Jack's expression. "A big move like this could set a healthy person to questioning. Someone with Alzheimer's?" He frowned as he swung the truck into a fairly tight space half a block beyond the church. "It's a lot to digest in a fairly short span of time.

But if we encourage him, and take it step by step, it might get better. I hope."

Liv hoped so, too, but the hectic hour before church had been a prime example of Grandma's concern the previous day. When Tom Mason didn't want to do something, he made his feelings known. She half dreaded going into the church of her youth, and not due to years of avoidance. That was between her and God.

Was Grandpa behaving or making a scene? Would the entire town be at the early service, watching her walk in with Jack? And would that ramp up the current gossip to a frenetic pace?

The carillon bells began chiming the bright opening thrums of Beethoven's *Ode to Joy*. The familiar music lightened her step, brightened her soul. She'd sung this countless times over the years, but it had been a long time since the music had called to her.

Today it did. As she entered the church, the softly lit interior reminded her of old days and new times. Jack came up alongside her and reached for her hand, a simple gesture of great magnitude in a small town like Jasper Gulch.

Liv drew a deep breath. Glanced up.

Sea-green eyes met hers, eyes that promised everything would be okay. She slipped her hand into his. The touch of his work-roughened palm felt good against her skin. The grasp of his fingers, twining with hers, combined old memories with new hopes, a perfect blend. And his look of promise, that everything would be fine, helped her believe.

They slid into a pew behind Liv's parents and grandparents. A young mother claimed the space to their right. Two busy, bright-eyed, new-to-walking toddlers clambered in with her, a mop-topped girl and a looking-for-mischief little fellow whose lopsided grin would surely break hearts one day.

The new pastor walked to the front of the church, ready to begin the morning service.

Bam! Bam! Bam! The little boy two-fisted his sippy cup against the aged wooden pew. His happy face reflected his delight at the loud, repetitive sound while droplets of milk sailed into the air with each strike. When his mother leaned over to caution him, he scowled at her, said a very loud and emphatic "NO!" and proceeded to hammer the pew again. *Bam! Bam! Bam!*

The young mother cajoled the cup from him, tucked it into a long-strapped bag, then turned to where the barely walking girl was trying to scale her mother's side in monkeylike fashion.

The little girl took one look up at her mother's frowning face and burst into tears.

Loud tears.

Liv reached over to tap the mother's arm, wondering if she could help in any way. The little girl saw the perfect stranger reaching in her direction and shrieked.

The mother turned quickly, her attention understandably torn. "Chrissy, what's—" She read the situation and tried to quickly apologize to Livvie. "She's afraid of people she doesn't know. But thank you—"

The words were barely out of her mouth when the little boy reconfiscated the cup from the quilted bag on the floor, turned it upside down and began dripping milk along the pew seat as if he was watering flowers in a garden, happy as could be. "Ya, ya, ya, ya…" His happy little voice caroled throughout the quiet church as the hapless mother tried to intervene once more.

"Whaa!" The little girl—Chrissy—seemed determined to outshriek her brother's singsong milk party. She quieted slightly when her mother turned attention her way, but began shrieking again when the little boy's antics required further intervention.

Half the church was watching the melee, the other half, well…they were behind Liv and she couldn't see them, but she figured they were most likely watching, too.

She'd worried about Grandpa causing a spectacle. He hadn't, so far he was being good as gold, but the racket set up by the two toddlers beat anything Grandpa might have done.

The young mother started crying, overwhelmed, grabbed both babies and fled down the aisle, the kids' angst echoing as she went.

The ensuing silence seemed harsh and surreal.

A young mother. Two small children. No father with them.

Could they have helped more? Done something else?

A tap on Liv's arm drew her attention around. Rosemary Middleton patted her shoulder, sent the now-quiet entrance a glance and offered comfort as she grabbed up her purse. "Hannah's had a rough go, Liv. A widow, so young, with twins. She's taken to staying home, staying put, because toddlers are an unpredictable handful. I was glad to see her come in, but now…" Her expression reflected the less than stellar outcome.

"Should I go help?" Liv asked.

"I'll go. The kids know me from the store."

She slipped out as the pastor began the service with a smile of gratitude in Rosemary's direction. He didn't seem put out or disgruntled by the initial ruckus, nor did he make a joke about kids and behavior. From the look on the young mother's face—Hannah—there was nothing amusing about the situation from her point of view, and Liv appreciated the minister's sensitivity. Sitting behind her beloved grandfather, she knew that next time it might be him stirring up a fuss. Sensitivity for the old, the young and the troubled took on new importance to her these days.

Thankfully, her worries for the day went unfounded. Grandpa Mason was the soul of good behavior, and Grandma seemed happy to be in church again, surrounded by family.

"Kind of nice, isn't it?" Jack whispered the words as they stood to sing a final hymn. He indicated her aging grandparents with a dip of his chin. "Despite the hardships, I think Grandma and Grandpa are still in love, even after all this time."

They were. It showed in the gentle way Grandma helped adjust Grandpa's prayer book, the way she held the book of hymns just so, allowing Grandpa to see the words at his own level.

Their actions exampled the promise of "in sickness and health." Despite Grandpa's poor prognosis, Grandma stuck by his side, rarely showing her frustration. And that was a lesson Liv needed, no, *wanted* to learn.

And when the sweet service was complete, Jack stepped out of the pew, allowing Livvie to move before him. He didn't take her hand on the way out, and that made her wish he would, her fingers longing to be threaded with his again.

"Jack." The young minister grinned as she and Jack came into the church foyer. The propped doors bled sunshine into the entry, flooding the floor with golden light. "Good morning! Let me know if you need another practice before the game next weekend. I've been reshaping my glove, getting it ready."

Jack laughed. "I should do the same thing. Mine has been sitting on a closet shelf for a lot of years. Ethan, this is Olivia Franklin."

"Dave and Jane's daughter, right?"

Liv nodded, surprised. "How did you know that?"

Ethan aimed a funny face of disbelief toward Main Street and splayed his hands as if to say how could he *not* know that?

Liv burst out laughing. "So you understand that there are no secrets in Jasper Gulch. That's the first step toward survival, Reverend Johnson."

He shook his head and clasped her hand in welcome. "First, call me Ethan, please. Second, I figured it out the minute the knitters and ladies' auxiliary and Daughters of the West discovered I was single. I have been the subject of ardent guesswork about the future Mrs. Ethan Johnson from that moment."

"Which means random folks dropping off casseroles, banana bread, cream-cheese brownies and cookies to showcase kitchen skills."

Ethan's grin said she was correct. "I've tried to tell them that all is accomplished in God's time. But there are a few who long to give the Good Lord whatever help they can."

Liv knew that firsthand. She'd seen the raised brows when she and Jack walked in. The quickly hidden smiles. Looks of surprise.

But she'd noticed something else, too.

The combined reactions didn't seem nosy today. They seemed happy to see her and Jack together. Maybe pleased by the easy look on Jack's face? The more joyful appearance he had now? That wasn't a bad thing, to inspire joy in others.

You will draw water joyfully from the springs of salvation.

Ethan's gentle preaching had cited joyful texts in the Bible, words of affirmation in times of hardship.

She'd forgotten how many there were. Silly of her, to dwell on the negatives instead of embracing the positives in life. Was thirty too old to grasp that change?

Regrasp it, you mean. Because you used to love the joys in life. You grabbed hold and ran with them until Jack dumped you. So who's more guilty here? Him for being stupid? Or you for letting someone else's choice chart your destiny for eight long years?

"Ethan, would you like to catch breakfast with us?" Jack asked the question easily as if sharing a table with Liv was the norm, maybe because it had been normal for so long.

Ethan refused, regretful. "I'd love to another day, but I've got Sunday school in a few minutes and it's my turn to preside. Then I'm heading to Bozeman to do a hospital visit. This stretch of heat is tough on the elderly."

"And if you're gone midday on Sunday, it limits the number of people who can invite you to dinner to meet their eligible daughters."

Ethan's lips quirked in acknowledgment. "Timing is everything. Liv, nice to meet you." He reached out to shake Liv's hand as her parents and grandparents came through the door behind them. "And, Jack, I'm looking forward to next Saturday." Ethan flexed his muscles, then cringed when his collar bit into his neck. "Reminder—no collars on the ball field."

"Although wearing it might get you preferential treatment from the umpires," Dave Franklin noted, grinning. "All's fair in love and baseball."

"I've ordered shirts for both teams, so the collar won't be an issue," Jack promised. He clapped a hand to Ethan's shoulder. "Nice service, Ethan. Again." Jack moved toward the beam of light. When he reached back for Liv's hand, the look on his face...

Tender, caring, loving...

Gave her the answer she'd been looking for.

She didn't want to leave Jasper Gulch, and truth to tell, she didn't need to leave right away. Jack's face, his expression, the affection in his eyes, said everything.

She'd stay right here and figure things out. As Mert said, sometimes things were just too important to yack about, and whatever this was between her and Jack McGuire needed time. She'd be wrong to shortchange that and she was tired of making mistake upon mistake. She had the university-job interview set up for tomorrow morning. If she took the position, she'd commute for the year. A lot of folks had long commutes in cities. If bad weather curtailed her on occasion, she'd face that as it came. "You ready to feed me, cowboy?"

"Ready and willing. And I do like those shoes, Liv. A lot."

She caught his teasing look and laughed, remembering her angst over the shoes before church but the favorable look marking Jack's glance to her legs, her feet?

Made the cute heels worth every moment of finding the proper skirt without too many wrinkles.

Chapter Thirteen

❧

Robin closed her laptop, stretched and yawned later that afternoon. "This is a wretched way to spend a summer Sunday, Liv. What are we thinking?"

"My eyes are bugging out, so I can't disagree." Liv stopped entering data, stood and finished her iced tea. "Do you want to walk to the creek?"

"No. You know what I really want to do? Really, truly?"

Liv didn't, so she shook her head. "No clue."

"I want to see a ranch. A real working ranch. With cowboys and cows and horses and well…did I mention cowboys?"

"You did." Liv laughed, glanced at the clock and nodded. "Hop in my car. I've got to take care of Dilly and the girls at the Double M. Which reminds me." She pulled out her phone and texted Jack that she wouldn't be around to care for the horses the following morning, but she'd make it up to them later in the day. "Come on, I'll give you a quick tour when we get there, but there probably won't be many cowboys around. Not midday on a Sunday."

"Am I dressed okay?" Robin wondered as Liv turned the car toward the McGuire ranch.

"For?"

Robin indicated her feet. "Aren't you supposed to wear boots on a ranch?"

"You're fine. For a city slicker."

"Grr."

"When there's more time, I'll loan you a pair of my boots and I'll bring you out to ride. We can saddle up the mares and get them used to being ridden again. If the heat breaks this week, we can start then. I bet you'd love it, Robin. Have you ridden before?"

"No, but I've always wanted to learn, almost as if it was born in me." Robin watched out the window as acres of tough Montana grassland swept by. "There's so much I want to know, Liv."

"About riding?" Liv slanted Robin a glance, curious, as she guided the car down the rolling lane leading to the McGuire house.

"About everything." Robin shrugged, but her face looked pensive. "Consider it the frustrated cowgirl within."

"Well, you've come to the right state to fix that, so let's start now." Liv stopped the car, climbed out and gave Robin a quick ranch overview. "Most of the cattle are pastured in the uplands on the far side of the McGuire ranch. A buyer purchased a dozen pregnant cows yesterday, but that leaves Jack and his dad with well over twelve hundred cattle running. Half are calves who'll get sold off late November."

"How big is this place?" Robin turned in a circle, then faced Liv. "It's huge, right?"

"Not like Shaw Ranch huge, but yeah. It's big. And worth a pretty penny. But Jack and his dad don't care about any of that."

Robin's face said that was hard to believe.

"Things are different in ranching families," Liv told her as she grabbed a lead for Dilly. She could give Robin a quick tour and offer the buckskin a walk around the ranch yard. Saying it, she began to realize the truth more deeply herself. "It's like you're part of the land. Born to it."

"But not everyone stays."

"No." Liv hooked her thumb toward the paddock housing Dilly and the mares. Jack had moved them in together the previous day, ready to acclimate the horses to their new reality. "It's not an easy life. Winter's cold, harsh and lasts way too long. Some years are real tough. But when you're a cowboy, well." She made a face, wishing she could explain but falling short. "It's part of you."

"You love it out here."

Liv grinned as she led Dilly out of the pen. "Is it that obvious?"

"Ridiculously so."

She reached out an arm to Dilly and gave him the neck rub he loved before handing the lead to Robin. "I think I'd do okay on a ranch. Jack's mother taught me a lot when I was younger. Hold the lead here while I finish the mares, okay?"

"Um. Sure." Robin made a face up at the big horse but kept her voice soft. "Did he look worse than this when you got him? Please say no."

"Much."

"Well, that just breaks my heart." Robin ran a hand along Dilly's neck and didn't cringe when loose hair came off on her fingers. Liv gave her extra points for that, and when she swiped the hand to the side of her jeans, Liv figured Robin might just make it in the West, after all. "What about your career?" Robin wondered.

"Maybe it's time to change things up. Or at least juggle a while. I'm trying to learn to trust God's timing. It's a big step for me."

Surprise and disbelief marked Robin's features. She sucked air between her teeth and cringed slightly. "That's a huge change, Liv. Don't you have an interview at the university tomorrow morning?"

"I do." Liv finished the mares' feed, then ran fresh water to the trough before taking the lead from Robin to exercise Dilly outside the pen. "And we'll see what happens with that. With all the changes in my family—"

"And the cute cowboy," Robin noted, indicating the sprawling Double M with a wave of her hand.

Liv smiled because the cute cowboy was a given. "I feel like I'm at a crossroads, with no red lights or stop signs, which means I have to pick a route and follow it. But no matter what I decide, we can continue to work together on the town history— unless you're getting ready to leave?"

Robin's profile said leaving was the last thing on her mind, but as she gazed outward at the ranch, she shrugged. "I'm a restless soul right now. Not sure what to do or where to go, I just know I want to feel like I belong somewhere. And I don't ever want to be lonely again. Pathetic, right?"

"Not at all," Liv answered, knowing loneliness wasn't just an issue when you were alone. Sometimes it happened in a busy office. Or a house built without true love. "No real roots back home, Robin?"

Robin made a face. "I was a fish out of water there, like my ancestors of old, the ones who may have traveled through here. So maybe that wanderlust passed on to me."

"We'll see how you feel about being here once winter's wrath keeps us cooped up for months." Liv raised her chin toward the endless mountains. "That's when ranch life makes you or breaks you. There's no cozy car heater on a 4X4 while you're checking fence. And the wind bites hard when you're monitoring newborn calves on horseback in ten degrees and biting wind."

"They have their babies outside? In the snow?" Robin stared at the mountains, then Liv, incredulous.

Liv laughed and gave her a friendly shoulder jab. "Welcome to ranching, my friend. And when it's calving time? Everyone helps, one way or another."

"I don't want to hear another bit about it," Robin told her. "I'm going to envision a manger scene, Christmas-friendly, a sweet cow, a bed of straw and a beautiful baby calf, all doe-eyed and clean."

"And I'll let you think that way, but the reality on a ranch is survival of the fittest. On the other hand, Jack and Mick take it quite personally if they lose a calf or cow." Liv remembered the stark look in Jack's eyes whenever a cow or calf went down, and that was another reason to love the McGuire men. Big men. Big hearts. "They see it as a failure, and it breaks their hearts."

"With twelve hundred cows?" Robin raised a brow in disbelief, as if caring for a huge number made the loss more understandable.

Liv knew better. She'd worked the ranch over a couple of college spring breaks. She understood the harsh conditions of early spring in the mountains, the bawling calves, snow barreling in on the heels of a Canadian clipper. And any time an animal succumbed, Mick, Jack and Mary Beth took it to heart. "A life's a life out here."

Robin reached up a hand to the needy horse clip-clopping alongside Liv. "You'll do okay here, Liv."

The possibility of sharing this life with Jack and

Mick made Liv see the possibilities before her more clearly. "I think I could, even after all that's gone on these past years. I'm just sorry it took me so long to realize it."

Jack's phone rang midmorning on Monday. He saw the bank manager's name and clicked in, surprised. "Mr. Thompson? What can I do for you?"

"Jack, that check from those folks in Decatur came back marked insufficient funds."

Jack stopped in his tracks because he'd talked his father into taking the personal check rather than insisting on a bank draft. And he'd only done that because he was familiar with the Brower legacy in Decatur, Nebraska. Their reputation, their stake in farming preceded them.

His heart sank.

Any farmer could run out of money, and many had the past few years. Would the Browers do that, though? Pass off a bad check and accept cattle without payment?

No.

At least he hoped they wouldn't. "Did you run it through again, Wilbur? Maybe funds got tied up between accounts."

"I called their bank personally because I didn't want to make this phone call, Jack. They said there aren't enough funds in their combined accounts to come close to covering a nearly twenty-thousand-dollar payment. I'm sorry."

He was sorry?

Oh, man. Jack scraped a hand to the nape of his neck to thwart the encroaching tension headache. "Not your fault, Wilbur. Mine for not insisting on a bank draft."

"They are the best way to go," Wilbur agreed, but Jack didn't want to hear that right then. He never took personal checks for big-business dealings. He'd learned that as a young man and had the practice reinforced as an investment adviser in Chicago. And this time of year, when money was tight on a ranch, waiting for that single big paycheck on "calves-to-market" day, well...

He bit down hard on a wad of gum, missed the gum and bit the inside of his cheek instead. Instant pain added to the financial blow. He'd been riding high these past few weeks, enjoying life for the first time in a long while. And now—

Now, what? So the Browers passed a bad check. You're runnin' off the deep end and you don't even know if it was intentional or inadvertent. Henry Brower's been in the business for decades, and his father before him. You really think he'd slip you a bad check and then waltz away with a trailerload of pricey, pregnant cows?

It wouldn't be the first time a farmer employed desperate means to get back on his feet. And it wasn't like the Browers lived next door. Going after the money would entail time, effort and distance, none of which Jack had right now. But whether or not he had the time, he had little choice because he'd made the decision to accept Henry's check. Now he'd have to man up and fix it. After admitting it to his father.

He shoved his hat aside, swept a wide hankie to his brow and continued checking fence. It was an all-day job in the middle of a heat wave, but making sure the Plow Creek pasture was tight and secure was his task of the day, and he wasn't about to mess that up after already messing up. He stopped to eat the sack of peanut-butter-and-jelly sandwiches he'd brought along and hit Liv's number on his speed dial.

The call went straight to voice mail, which was unusual. She rarely turned off her phone and frequently checked the battery to make sure it was charged. He dialed her parents' home instead. If she wasn't working with Robin, maybe she was back home, helping with Grandma and Grandpa. She'd texted him that she was busy this morning, but he didn't expect her to be unreachable. And with the financial smackdown he'd taken, hearing Liv's voice, her laugh, would ease the sting of handing over twenty thousand of his savings to the McGuire ranch fund.

"Trudy Mason here. Hello."

"Mrs. Mason, this is Jack McGuire. Liv's friend."

"Of course I know who you are, Jack. Liv's special friend." She put teasing emphasis on "special" as if to make a point. "What can I do for you?"

"Is Liv there? I tried her cell phone but it wasn't turned on."

"Oh, the interview, of course!" Grandma Mason exclaimed and then tsk-tsked modern technology. "She must have turned it off while she was interviewing for that job at the university in Bozeman."

Jack's heart sank again, only deeper this time. Much deeper.

Liv was interviewing for a job in Bozeman? And didn't tell him? "You're sure that's where she is, ma'am?"

"One hundred percent certain." The staunch note in the elderly woman's voice said she shouldn't be doubted. "She told me this morning she'd be at the interview and then shopping. Might as well get stuff bought and taken care of when you're in the city, right?"

Jack's heart deflated further.

He'd messed up his father's financials with misplaced trust, and that seemed to be the theme of the day because he never expected Liv to go off and get a job in the city—a city an hour's drive away in good weather—without making mention of it to him.

Doubts assailed him when he disconnected the call.

He thought they'd bridged a huge gap these past few weeks. When they were together, the last thing he wanted to do was leave her and head home, alone. When they were apart, he thought about her, nonstop. Right now his plans, hopes and dreams disappeared in a puff of reality smoke.

Liv might be leaving. Heading back to her life, her career. And he knew this would come, he'd expected as much initially, but that was before they'd had a chance to talk, laugh, kiss.

And oh, that kiss. A once-in-a-lifetime event, a moment of pure, ever-after sweetness, the kind of kiss that puts a man in mind of roots. Playgrounds. Porch swings.

He stared at the phone, hating how easy it was to find things out these days. In the old days he'd have been left to learn bad stuff in a much slower time frame. He'd have preferred that, because now he had the rest of the day working fence, alone, thinking of all he'd lost.

Money he could replace. It would be a stretch, but he'd banked a good deal in Chicago and his personal investments had paid off. It hurt, but the twenty-thousand loss wasn't a death knell for the ranch because he had the funds to cover it. But the thought of Liv leaving, when every part of his being longed for her to stay?

That broke his heart. He hadn't realized how much he'd assumed until her grandmother's easy words put him into his current tailspin.

Should he have spoken up sooner? Declared his intentions? And what were those, exactly? To tie a smart girl like Livvie up to a ranch kitchen, raising calves and kids, wasting the college degrees she'd worked so hard to get? How was that fair?

It's fair if that's where she wants to be, tweaked his conscience. *You might actually try asking the girl. See where that gets you. That's the sensible thing to do.*

Jack didn't want to be sensible. He didn't want to be turned down or pushed aside. He didn't want to be anyone's second choice. Not now. Not ever.

So that's it? You'll just up and let her go? It's only an hour away, for pity's sake. You don't have enough gumption to date a girl an hour away? Dude, you deserve to lose her if that's the extent of your limitations.

It wasn't the distance, Jack knew as he finally turned Roy-O back toward home.

It was desire.

Ranching was work, hard work, and if a marriage was to work on a ranch, it had to be 100 percent on all levels. Sure, folks worked off the ranch, more so these days than ever before. But a job an hour away, in the thick of winter?

He'd been born and raised in Montana blows. He understood the fury of storm after storm, and why driving an hour wasn't in anyone's best interests. And if Liv wasn't interested enough to stay here, with him?

Then maybe she hadn't forgiven him, after all.

Maybe their time together had been simply a sweet walk down memory lane.

His phone buzzed. He pulled it out, saw Liv's number and stared at the readout for long, drawn-out seconds. And then he turned the phone off and tucked it away.

Liv was smart and beautiful, she deserved the best God could offer her, and it certainly wasn't to waste her intelligence on a cattle ranch with someone who couldn't guard the bottom line. She deserved better than good. Liv Franklin deserved the best, and that wasn't him, a guy who failed to recognize a good thing when he had it. Whatever this job was, he couldn't justify asking her to miss an opportunity to shine as she was born to do, beauty and brains, a stellar package.

He rode easy down the hills later that afternoon, giving Roy-O a break, horse and rider both worn after a long day. And when the horse was cooled down, fed and put up for the night, Jack crossed the yard, let himself into the house and went to bed. Sleep was a long time in coming, and when it did, it came in fits and starts, with images of Livvie, Henry Brower and bad checks running together. He got up less rested than when he'd lain down, shrugged into the same dirty clothes he'd worn yesterday and hit the trail again. There was nothing and no one on the Plow Creek pasture to care how he looked, smelled or acted.

And today, that was just fine by him.

* * *

Whenever God closes a door, somewhere He opens a window. The old quote took shape when Abigail Rose called Livvie first thing Tuesday morning and offered her a job as the new curator of the under-construction museum. "We can't pay too much, and it's really part-time for starters, but Livvie, if you're staying in Jasper Gulch, Chauncey and I think you'd be perfect for the job."

"And the mayor approved?" That seemed more surprising than anything. She and Jackson Shaw hadn't seen eye to eye on too many things.

"When it comes to history, Chauncey and I usually get our way." Abigail's tone said it was a given in history matters, and knowing Chauncey Hardman, Liv didn't doubt it. "Abigail, I'd love to take the position. And part-time is perfect right now. Thank you!"

"None needed. We're lucky to have someone of your caliber, Liv, and we know that," Abigail assured her. "And if you don't mind my asking, what shade of polish were you wearing on Friday? I'm not big on blue nails, it doesn't seem quite right, but I did like the color you had on."

"Teal Stencil," Liv replied. "It's one of my favorite summer shades."

"I'll check it out," declared Abigail. "Mind you stop by my office to get the applications for employment forms in the next day or two, okay?"

"I will. And Abigail?"

"Yes?"

"Thank you."

Abigail's soft laugh came through loud and clear. "Welcome home, Livvie Franklin."

"Have you seen Jack?" Liv approached Mick as he pulled his pickup truck into the ranch yard about an hour later.

"Not today. He was up and out early. Didn't see him yesterday, either, but the dust in the kitchen said he'd been through there."

"Men," she scolded, laughing. "Dust stays outside. That's what porches and mudrooms are for. I could have emailed him this stuff, but he said your printer was giving you a hard time this past week, so I thought I'd print these off and leave them here when I tended the horses. And I told Robin Frazier I'd teach her to ride if the heat breaks this week like they're predicting. Is that all right?"

"I'd be obliged." Mick strode next to her as they approached Dilly's pen. "The mares were a good buy. I look at them and I see Mary Beth's dreams for this ranch coming to life. Both beauties, ready to breed. Long as you don't mind spending some time babying them."

"My pleasure." Liv ducked through the rail and grinned back at Mick when Dilly didn't shy away. Instead, he moved closer, plodding toward her in a show of trust. "Sweet difference, right?"

"Yes, it is." Mick raised a handful of mail and the

notes Livvie brought along. "I'll put these inside, then pick up Maggie and Brian from their friend's place. Carrie's car is in the shop again."

"Cars are like plumbing and computers," Liv agreed as she led Dilly forward for an easy walk around the yard. "They're great when they work. If I miss Jack, will you see that he gets those, please?"

"Will do. But I can't believe you won't be seeing him later today."

She hoped so. And she hoped she'd see him tomorrow, and the next day, and the one after that, ad infinitum. How perfectly was this all working out?

Jack, her Jack. A job at the museum. A chance to help with Grandma and Grandpa. But right now, she needed to get the horses cared for and head for City Hall, excited to see Jack later.

Except she didn't.

He didn't call that day. Or the next. And when she called him to see if something was wrong, her call went straight to voice mail.

Was he avoiding her?

Impossible. They'd been having so much fun together, such a wonderful time, and those moments when their eyes met? Their hands touched?

The tenderness in Jack's gaze made her long to jump into life with Jack, no hesitation. And that was a big change from the timid, hands-off girl who drove into town a month before.

He's turned tail and run before, her conscience

scolded. *I do believe I warned you of that. You, of course, chose not to listen.*

Liv shushed the negative voice. She wouldn't listen now, either, not when she finally felt right with life. With love.

Was she foolish to trust him, after what happened last time?

Maybe. But sitting by his side in church, sensing his smile as she tried to calm a curly-haired little girl, made her see the deeper side of Jack McGuire. Kind, yes. Honest to a fault. And self-sacrificial. He'd go the distance to help someone out. A heart of gold with a rancher's singular mindset. A good combination, all told.

But when he hadn't called by Thursday, she wondered if she'd made the wrong leap of faith again. She stared at her phone Thursday afternoon, willing it to ring.

It didn't. And when Robin wondered what was wrong, she tried to shrug it off and failed.

"No call, no contact, no nothing? Since Monday?" Robin squared off as if ready to fight for her new friend's honor. "You left messages?"

"Several times."

"And got no response?"

Liv sighed, not wanting to talk about it yet longing to share with someone. How funny to be sharing her feelings with Robin Frazier, the one person in town who hadn't known her backstory with Jack from years before. "I can't believe I've been stupid again."

"You haven't, Liv. You've—" Liv's scowl got Robin to be quiet, but not for long. "I'm shocked. Amazed. And downright angry."

Her zeal made Liv smile, despite herself. "Robin. You barely know him. And you can't be mad at him. He hasn't done anything except possibly break my heart. Again. I should be used to it by now. Although at least he had a reason the last time. Or so he thought. But this is exactly what he did then, employing 'radio silence,' which I now refer to as pouting."

"If the description fits," Robin growled, clearly upset for her new friend. "I don't get it." She stormed around the cell-size space, trying to keep her voice down and failing.

Great. Now the entire town would be privy to Liv's romantic foibles again. Three swings at love? And three strikes. She was "out" now, by anyone's game. Time for a change of subject. Past time, actually. "Did you find anything in your searches that would indicate why our blonde, husband-hunting, ice-cream-counter girl might be involved in the disappearance of the capsule?"

"Nothing." Robin shook her head and made a face. "Lilibeth might have Available for Marriage stamped on her forehead, but Capsule Thief?" She negated that thought instantly. "No way."

At least they were in full agreement on that score.

Liv mentally scanned her choices as packed up for the day. Should she ride out to the ranch and take care of the horses? She'd made a promise, but after days of not hearing from Jack—and thinking she might run into him and how awkward that would be—it made her second-guess the task at hand. But a promise was a promise. Even so, she wouldn't deny the apprehension building inside as the days slid silently by. Memories converged, mounting an attack on her trust, her newfound faith, her already damaged ego. Could he be doing the same thing again? The signs pointed to yes.

Would he?

Her heart said no, but she hadn't been able to trust her heart for a long time.

Go see him. Force the confrontation. Get it over with, once and for all.

The stern voice within didn't want to be shushed, but Liv hushed it anyway. She didn't want a confrontation. She didn't want drama. She wanted sweet old-fashioned faith, hope and love.

She drove to the ranch, uncertain about a lot of things, but sure of one: she was in love with Jack McGuire and this time she'd stick to her guns. No knee-jerk replacements, no foiled attempts at love. She'd learned that lesson the hard way, but she'd learned it and had no desire to repeat the painful process. Although at least last time they'd had the gift of distance to lessen the pain. Now, with her new job as the museum curator?

Her worst fears had come true, that Jack would dump her and they'd be stuck in the same town together, nodding politely when they passed on the street.

Grim, she aimed the car for the Double M, determined to get on with things, one way or another. And if she ran into Jack McGuire there?

Homicide might not be ruled out.

Jack tapped on Liv and Robin's closet-turned-office door a few minutes later that afternoon. When he poked his head in, there was no sign of Liv. Disappointment nailed him, which meant his decision to let her find her own way wasn't sitting well. "Robin? Is Liv here?"

Robin looked surprised to see Jack when she first turned around. And then?

Oh, then she looked downright aggravated as she marched across the narrow room, her eyes boring into his. "Shame on you, Jack McGuire. Shame, shame, shame!"

"Huh?" He pulled back, surprised, amazed and not a little worried because Robin's face said she was ready to do battle and he was the only other combatant in the room.

"Leading a nice girl like Livvie on, getting her all excited over falling in love with you, wanting to be with you, have sweet little babies with you and then you go and do this!"

Him? Livvie? Babies? "Robin. Slow down. What in the name of Sam Hill are you talkin' about, woman?"

"Olivia Franklin, that's what I'm talking about!"

"Shh." Jack grimaced, turned and shut the door behind him, but he was pretty sure the dead silence from the front desk of the town offices meant all ears were tuned to their rather loud conversation. Which meant they needed to tone it down. "I don't know what you mean."

"You don't?" She came right up to him and raised her hand in the air, her gaze locked with his as she popped her fingers up, one by one. "You take a girl out, get her all moony-eyed over your ranch, buy her a horse, let her play with puppies, and then, after she's helped you put together a great hometown baseball game geared toward a good cause, you turn tail and run. That's what, Jack McGuire. And if you're not ashamed of yourself—" she folded her arms across her chest and tapped one ominous foot on the floor, *tap, tap, tap* "—I'm ashamed enough for both of us and I barely know you."

"That would have been my next point," Jack muttered, scrubbing a hand to his neck. "Listen, Robin, I know you mean well, but it's not like that with me and Liv. I mean, I thought it was. I hoped it was. But then she got this really good job in the city, and what kind of guy holds a woman back from an opportunity like that? What kind of a jerk do you think I am?"

"Job? What job?"

So she didn't know, either. Jack hauled in a

breath and came clean. "Liv got a job at the Bozeman campus of Montana State University. On Monday."

"Who told you this?" Robin studied his face as he answered, and he was pretty sure the ponytailed blonde might have missed her calling. Surely the FBI could use another skilled interrogator.

"Her grandmother."

"Ah." The toe resumed tapping, but not as slow and threatening as it had been before. This tap was a little more rhythmic and snappy. "So you took the word of a somewhat rattled septuagenarian and wrote Liv off without talking to her, asking her questions or approaching her in any way, shape or form. Is that how Western guys do it? Because no wonder it takes you guys forever to find a wife."

"Hey, I—" Jack stopped, replayed the conversation in his head, then angled his chin down. "Do you mean she didn't get the job offer?"

"Of course she did, you big dork, they'd have been crazy not to offer her a position with a résumé like hers."

"Then, I don't—"

Robin refused to give him a chance to finish. "They offered. Liv turned it down."

"She… Say what?"

"She refused their offer. She apologized for wasting their time and said she needed to stay in Jasper Gulch for a while. That she had unfinished business here. Namely, you, I think, but she didn't say that to the department head. At least not outright."

"She refused the job." The thought of Liv turning down a good job like that spurred a mix of emotions, but in the end, joy won out. "She's staying here? Really?"

"A fact you'd know if you got your head out of the pasture and talked to her. Are all cowboys this addled and dense?" she wondered aloud, but a growing smile took some bite out of her words. "Because if this is the norm—" she pointed to him and her voice said it wasn't exactly a compliment "—I'm steering clear of cowboys once and for all."

"Where is she now?" he asked. He glanced at his watch and frowned. "She's at my place, isn't she?"

"Very Shakespearean, star-crossed lovers, complete with the melodrama we all know and love," Robin told him. "Yes, she's there taking care of your animals and probably fit to be tied because you've been ignoring her for days."

"Well, that's over," Jack promised. He reached out and hugged a very surprised Robin, then turned and hurried out the door. "I'm heading home."

He pulled into the yard abutting the near barn just as Liv approached her car. She looked up. Saw him. And the look on her face, the expression of angst and sadness, rolled into one, made him want to beat himself up. He came to a stop just shy of her car and bounded out of the truck. He closed the distance between them in record speed and grabbed two very surprised hands in his. "You're staying."

Liv stared up at him, pulled her hands free and rounded the side of the car. "Actually, I'm going home to make supper for Grandma and Grandpa." She started to climb into the driver's seat, but Jack stepped between her and the car.

"I mean here. You're staying in Jasper Gulch."

Liv looked up again, and her expression said this wasn't news. "That's been the intent right along, hasn't it?"

"Wait, stop, Liv. Talk to me. Didn't you go to Bozeman on Monday for a job interview?"

She nodded and shrugged. "For a job I decided I didn't want and shouldn't have applied for."

"You turned down their offer."

A slow look of awareness deepened the light blue of her eyes to a stormy gray. "You thought I was leaving."

"Your grandmother said you were leaving, taking a job in Bozeman."

Liv's gaze cut through him. "You thought I was leaving and so you ignored me for three long days. Three very long days."

"Liv, I—" He jumped in, ready to explain about the bad check and his lack of faith, but she cut him off right sharp.

"Don't." She put up a hand, palm out, fingers splayed, a clear stop sign. "You didn't trust me enough to ask, or care enough to consider a long-distance relationship. You took it upon yourself to pout and get angry all over again, and Jack?" She turned her attention toward the ranch, the horses, the distant trees, hills and mountains and shook her head. "I can't do this. I can't deal with your lack of trust. I get that life hands out disappointments, but I thought you grew up. I thought *we* grew up. Looks like I was wrong." She pointed left, giving him no choice but to move out of the way, because she was right.

He'd reacted without giving her a chance to explain herself and all because he'd taken a financial blow. He'd jumped to conclusions, wishing she'd stay, then deciding he had nothing of import to offer a smart, educated woman like her because he was mad at himself again.

She got into the car, shaking her head, her features rigid.

He'd hurt her. He'd made assumptions and acted on them, and that wasn't husband material. That was lack of faith talking. In himself and in God's timing. And that lack of faith might have just cost him the most precious thing in the world, again.

Olivia Franklin.

Heat lightning sparked along the distant mountains. Jagged flashes crimped the federal-blue sky, the light casting shades of gray in its wake.

Jack thought she was going. He'd assumed the worst and instead of talking to her, facing her, he'd tucked tail and crawled into his hermit-rancher cave, much as he'd done before.

Liv's heart broke all over again. She'd felt so good being here. Whole. Alive. And she'd blossomed in the light of a growing faith, a hope that sprang from within. God's hope.

She didn't feel very hopeful now. Angry?

Yes.

Disappointed?

Check!

Miserable?

She stuck her lower lip out, much like little Chrissy had done in church, then drew it back in when the resemblance seemed too obvious.

She'd done a lot of growing lately, but not enough, it seemed. Because right now she wanted to throw one of those little-kid hissy fits, stomp her feet, fold her arms across her chest and scowl.

She didn't.

Instead, she turned the car left, headed for the wood-and-stone church, parked, climbed out and tried the door, fully expecting it to be locked at suppertime on a Thursday.

The church door swung open easily. The scent of old wood and new oil teased her senses. She crept in, found the pew she'd shared with Jack, sank down and prayed. She prayed for understanding. For faith. For wisdom, because she hadn't felt all that smart of late. And when she was done praying, she sat quietly, seeping in the silence, letting peace flow through her.

She was a child of God, a princess of the Most High King. No matter what happened with her and Jack, she'd done the right thing turning down the teaching position. Being here, working in the museum she helped raise money for, felt right. She could assist with Grandpa. Give Grandma some much-needed free time. And she could get to know her grandparents all over again. This time, she'd accept God's time and use it wisely.

She stood to leave as a handful of choir members came in the back entrance. They smiled at her. One of the older fellows removed his cap, the old-style dignity a sweet pleasure. "Good day, Miss Livvie."

"And to you." She eased out the door, into the light of an oblique sun, the days growing shorter as August wound down. She breathed deep, squared her shoulders and headed home, ready to begin this new stage of her life, letting God's light brighten her way.

She'd turned down a good-paying job, committed herself to being in Jasper Gulch and lost the man she loved, but with God's help, she'd turn it all around.

Although the thought of being a town spinster didn't sit well, so she pushed that image aside and went home. She had work to do tomorrow, and then the big game on Saturday.

A game with Jack, surrounded by baseball. Fun.

Liv ignored the droll tone of her conscience and decided she would have fun. If nothing else, she was helping the town she loved, and for that reason alone, she'd plant a smile on her face and work the game she'd planned at his side.

Only, she'd work it without acknowledging Jack McGuire's presence on the planet, very Austen friendly. That realization meant she might need a little more faith formation in the forgiveness area. And she'd be happy to work on that, after Saturday's game.

You blew it. Again.

The harsh scolding from Jack's conscience was nothing he didn't already know.

What was wrong with him? What was he thinking, going off half-cocked over something as simple as money?

In your defense, it wasn't exactly pocket change.

Jack shrugged off the lame excuse. Twenty grand was significant funding, but the money wasn't the problem.

He was the problem.

He strode across the gravel drive, fingers twitching, longing for forgiveness—and a fight.

Blue yipped from the kennel on the back porch. Jack tried to ignore the pup's whine, but the little fellow fussed again, scraping the front of his cage with tiny paws, needing to have a run around the yard.

Jack changed direction, moved to the porch and released the little heeler from the dog-training crate. "Come on out here, boy."

The pup didn't need encouragement. He bounded down the steps after Jack, scurrying about, spinning here and there, sniffing possible target areas, anxious until he'd taken care of the necessities of puppy life. Then he came and sat at Jack's feet, his mottled face upturned, tongue out, panting happy emotion, his tiny tail thumping a beat of pure love.

Mick pulled in just then. He rolled to a stop, saw Jack and the pup, and smiled. "I was thinking he'd need a spell around the yard about now and didn't know you were here. Hey, Blue."

The pup dashed toward Mick, thrilled to have both men on board. Mick picked up the puppy, cradled him and eyed Jack. "You've looked better."

Jack grimaced because he knew it was true.

"And I passed Livvie's car on my way here, so I'm guessing you're in the doghouse for something."

"I think it's beyond the doghouse," Jack admitted. "She pretty much wants to be done with me."

"Well, we men aren't the brightest creatures in the world," Mick acknowledged as he smoothed one hand across the pup's head and back. "And we mess up continually. Somehow we manage to put other things first, in front of our women. Your mother wasn't afraid to call me on it. Fairly often."

Jack cringed. "So it's a family trait? Great."

Mick laughed. "Some of us learn faster than others. What did you do?"

"Acted stupid. She had a chance at a big job in Bozeman and I thought staying here with a guy like me would be unfair, so I backed off."

"You wanted the best for her." Mick shrugged one shoulder, considering Jack's words. "Nothing wrong with that, Jack. But when we try to make decisions for women, deciding what's in their best interests? That's when we stir up a pot of trouble." He set Blue down, gave a whistle and moved toward the back barn. "I'm going to let him run around out back a bit. I'm having supper at Carrie's tonight with the kids, so you're on your own."

On his own. Alone, again. Because he'd done exactly what his father said, he'd made decisions for Liv while mad at himself.

When would he grow up, for real? Learn to trust God, trust Livvie, trust that life would work itself out?

Dilly padded across the corral, a light breeze sifting the horse's mane as he moved. He tossed his head, showing off, a sure sign of improved health and humor. The neglected steed had come back to life under Livvie's gentle, skilled hands, her patient nature. Her proficiency on the ranch was right before him, in plain sight. Why hadn't he weighed the importance of that, how she loved being here? Working here? Getting dirty right alongside him?

Love is patient, love is kind...

The popular verse from Corinthians made Jack rethink his actions.

He'd been so proud of his baseball career, his successes. When his injury stopped them cold, he reacted badly. When his mother passed away, he kept himself to the ranch, running herd and working off his grief in silence. And when he realized he'd made a bad risk on a twenty-thousand-dollar debt, he'd tucked tail again, not wanting Liv tied to a failure.

Love is patient, love is kind...

He hadn't been patient or kind. He'd been quietly foul-tempered, ready to pack his toys and go home like a spoiled kid, refusing to look at the big picture. His mother used to look at the good and bad in life, shrug and say, "And this, too, will pass."

He needed to do that more often. Accept the bad times, enjoy the good and deal with life like a responsible adult. Like Livvie, he realized, and that deepened his regret.

He moved to the house, determined to make it up to her, someway, somehow. If he needed to grovel, he'd grovel. If he needed to beg, well...

He scrubbed a hand to the back of his neck, growled and sighed, then decided, yes. If he needed to beg, he'd beg, because letting Livvie go a second time would make him the stupidest guy in Big Sky country and he'd already done that once.

He really didn't want to do it again.

Chapter Fourteen

"**Y**ou're bound to see him today." Jane Franklin noted Saturday morning as she double-checked for sunscreen and Grandpa's hat. Halfway through the big game he might decide one or the other wasn't working. Getting his scalp sunburned wouldn't be in anyone's best interests.

"Then I'll see him from a distance," Liv declared. She thumped around the kitchen, agitated at the thought of being elbow-to-elbow with Jack throughout this day. She gathered supplies into her bag to help ensure a great time would be had by all, when she was about to have the worst day of her life.

She and Jack, working together, pretending things were all right in front of a thousand or so onlookers, half of whom would talk up the events of the day nonstop for the coming week.

She didn't want or need to be a spectacle. Not now. Not ever.

"Liv?"

The sound of Jack's voice at the kitchen door hard-stopped her heart.

"May I come in?"

"Sure." Jane sent Liv a scolding frown Jack couldn't see, leaned over and pushed the wooden screen door his way. "I'm going to go check on Grandma and Grandpa. They're very excited about the game today, Jack."

"Good. I'm glad." His words sounded perfunctory, and that was probably because the look he settled on Liv was steadfast and unhappy, a tough mix. "I came to apologize." He'd taken off his baseball cap and fiddled with the brim while he spoke. "I made a fool of myself and I've got no one but myself to blame for it. I jumped to conclusions—"

"And pouted."

He sucked in a breath, then agreed, his gaze troubled. "Like a five-year-old. Yes. But it wasn't about you leaving, at least not just that." He paused as his phone buzzed, then frowned, clearly unhappy about taking the call, but it was game day, after all, and Jack would be a busy man. "Wilbur. Can I call you back?"

Whatever Wilbur said on the other end lightened Jack's features considerably. In fact, by the time he ended the call, he wore a broad smile, which meant he might not bow and scrape as much as he should after being a complete dork for days. Liv wasn't sure how to feel about that. Provoked and incensed seemed just about right.

Jack held the phone up. "That phone call solved the first part of my problem, one that was caused by a banking error someplace in Nebraska, a simple mistake that misplaced a twenty-thousand-dollar deposit last week, but that's no excuse for me being out-and-out dumb, Liv. And bullheaded."

She kept her expression flat and motioned with her hand that he should continue the list because dumb and bullheaded were a "barely-scratched-the-surface" beginning.

"Wilbur called me Monday to say a check had bounced. A big one. I'd pushed my father to take the check and when it bounced, I was pretty sure I was the biggest loser in Montana. And then your grandma said you were taking a job in Bozeman and all I could see was the opportunity they were handing you. A chance to be someone special, to use all that education, to climb that ladder of success the way we all knew you should. That sounded so much better than being bound up in Jasper Gulch with a loser like me."

"So you ignored me and wouldn't talk to me because you were pouting and being self-sacrificial?" Liv crossed her arms over her chest and made sure Jack read the glare she shot him. "Not to mention boneheaded?"

"All three?" He said the words cautiously, as if

unsure of the right answer, and he was wise to do so because there was no right answer.

Liv moved forward. "Your communication skills are appalling, cowboy."

His face said he knew that.

"And that's not acceptable in life, in love. In marriage."

His eyes widened, but there might have been the tiniest ray of hope behind the surprise she saw there.

"But this isn't the time or the place to talk about any of this." She picked up a tote and shoved it at him, then gathered the bag she'd packed to keep things straight all day. "We've got a game to play."

"We'll talk later?"

She studied him, then the bright August day outside, then nodded. "Later."

"Then let's play ball, Liv."

She followed him to his truck, tempted to take a stand and insist on driving herself, but the truth was, she wanted to be with Jack in the big 4X4 pickup. Did that make her pathetic?

It makes you a woman in love. Just make sure you're on the same page this time, okay?

She mentally agreed with the sage advice, knowing she'd come a long way in eight years and determined that this time, with the grace of God, she'd land on her feet. And that decision felt more than good. It felt great.

* * *

"Jack, we've got a problem." Coach Randolph moved toward them as Jack pulled into a parking spot behind the small grandstand. "Someone got into the storeroom last night. We've got equipment missing."

"How'd they get in?" Jack spotted the cut padlock and whistled tightly between his teeth. "They nipped the padlock?"

"Yes. And we're missing the catcher's equipment, the extra bats, the anchored bases and the microphone set-up."

"Who would do such a thing?" Liv wondered as she approached from the other side of the truck. "And why?"

"That's the question right there," Coach agreed. He raised his cell phone, indicating the time. "I can get to my place and grab some backup catcher equipment, but it will take a while."

"Is there a problem?" Hutch Garrison ambled up to the group, and Jack fully expected to experience the normal crawl of envy up his spine. As a Colorado Rockies center fielder, Hutch was living the dream Jack had worked so hard for back in the day, but as Hutch approached, looking concerned, Jack felt none of the old angst.

Coach started to explain, but Sonny Munoz trotted in and motioned to the family's patched-up car. "Coach, I've got Brad's catcher equipment in the trunk. He had to go straight to work after the last game and he needed someone to stow it. My trunk was handy. Will that help?"

"It sure would, and it would save me an hour round trip," the coach declared. "I've got the portable bases in my van. They'll do fine for today."

"Extra bats won't be a problem." Jack pulled a sack of his personal bats out of the back of the truck. "Figured these should finally see the light of day again." He caught the look of approval on Liv's face, and the tiny ray of hope from earlier grew into a faint beam. Not that he was taking anything for granted, no sir, not after acting like a first-class jerk for days. "But a microphone. Where can we get a microphone set-up?"

Cord Shaw had come up from the parking lot in time to hear the last sentence. He nodded to Coach and pulled out his cell phone. "We have a set-up we used for the rodeo gig last month. If my brother Austin hasn't left the house yet, I'll have him bring it along. Adam's already on his way with some special order you had him pick up?" He aimed the question at Jack.

"Then we're okay," Jack announced. Adam would be here with the game shirts, and Cord would get the sound system up and running. They had bases, bats and enough players to man two teams. There were no replacements, but for a fun, one-time-deal kind of game, they really didn't need any. He took a breath and offered the group a nod of confidence. "Let's do this."

As the players dispersed, Jack stopped Hutch Garrison with a hand to his arm. "Hutch. It's truly nice to meet you and thanks so much for taking the time to be with us this morning."

"My pleasure." Hutch shook Jack's hand and skimmed the field a glance. "I chased a lot of your records on this field."

"And caught one."

"Yeah." Hutch shrugged that off. "I'm sorry you got hurt, man. You'd have been great."

His words made Jack pause, the thoughts of what could have been a former constant in his head. Now?

Not so much. "Stuff happens. And I'm here now, with my father. A ranch I love. Riding herd, mending fence. Things worked out."

Sonny Munoz trotted back from the parking lot with the sack of catcher's equipment. Jack took the moment to introduce the rising star to Jasper Gulch's current baseball hero. "Sonny, this is Hutch Garrison."

The kid gulped, grinned and stuck out his hand. He managed to bump Jack with the awkward bag of equipment, then stopped, embarrassed. "Boss, I—"

"It's fine, kid. Why don't you get Hutch set up in his area, make sure he's got coffee, water, pens and programs to sign. Let's make some money for the future of Jasper Gulch, okay?"

"Yes, sir. I will." Sonny led Hutch to the shaded booth on the perimeter of the field, not far from where the Sports Boosters were firing up the grill for hamburgers and hot dogs. To his left, the ladies' auxiliary baked-food sale was being arranged. Just beyond the rows of spice cakes and peach pies, Jack saw Liv making sure the baseball-memorabilia vendors each had space for their goods. Having them come on board for a nominal "booth fee" had been Liv's idea, and from the growing enthusiasm around them, folks had come from all over to see some baseball and spend some money. And that meant revenue raised for the bridge and the museum.

"Jack, I just wanna thank you for stepping up to the plate like you did." Wes Middleton approached him from the near side of the bleachers. "I don't know what we'd've done if you hadn't taken the reins when I got sick. Rosemary and I are real appreciative."

"I couldn't have done it this well without Liv's help." Jack made sure she heard his compliment, even though she was a dozen feet away, checking on the Sports Boosters. "She and Rusty kept me on track."

"Mostly her." Rusty approached them with a grin, and hooked a thumb in Liv's direction. "I was pretty sure the whole thing was dead in the water, then she come to town and it's amazin' how quick Jack perked up with a purty girl around."

Liv's smile said she approved Rusty's words, but Jack wasn't taking anything for granted. He'd messed up, and no matter what effort it took on his part, he was going to make things up to Liv. If he got his way, she'd never spend another day wondering about his love and devotion. That's if he could get her to start talking to him again. Without the narrow-eyed glare and scolding tone she'd used on Thursday, a combination he deserved then.

Now?

He wanted another chance at the gold ring he'd missed the first time around.

The baked-food sale was open for business with a growing array of cookies, pies, cake slices and every kind of Midwestern "bar" Liv could imagine. A nut-topped peach pie called to Liv, but a plate full of chocolate-chip cookies won out as her first purchase of the day. If Jack didn't shape up in quick form, then drowning her sorrows in a dozen homemade cookies couldn't be considered a *bad* thing.

The hamburger stand was up and running, tempting everyone with the scent of fresh, hot burgers and hot dogs. The smell of shoestring fries mixed with the grilling meat, a total baseball sensation. The Jasper Gulch Hose Company had their chicken-barbecue pit filled with slow-burning wood. Soon the air would be tinged with the scent of barbecuing chicken, a summer smell for sure. And the soda booth was already doing a bang-up business with the morning-coffee crowd. Chauncey Hardman had had the good sense to bring along her coffee system, and from the looks on folks' faces, she'd made a big hit. Coffee, hot and strong, helped form the backbone of Montana ranchers. Chauncey did well to remember that.

"Liv, we're here!"

Grandma Mason's voice hailed her from the far side of the bleachers. She waved and Grandma waved back, but when she tried to point Liv out to Grandpa, confusion clouded her grandfather's face. At home he was doing okay. Out here, surrounded by people he didn't know in a place he'd never seen, the old gentleman seemed out of his element. Until he turned and saw Sonny Munoz attaching bases to the field.

Grandpa's shoulders straightened. His chin came up. A broad smile split his face, and he raised both hands to his mouth and hollered, "Batter up!"

Not one person minded that it wasn't quite time to start the day's festivities. Most looked as if they appreciated the old man's enthusiasm, because in Jasper Gulch, Montana, the heart of football country, everyone loved baseball.

The stands filled over the next twenty minutes. Cars streamed in from the single road leading to the interstate, and locals walked, biked and drove in from the other directions.

The popcorn booth added its come-and-get-me aroma to the game day delights, and as Liv watched the players begin to gather in the dugouts, a sense of awareness swept her. She'd been to many a game on this field, watching Jack play, and she and Mary Beth had gone to games in various towns a dozen years back. Since then? So much had changed, hearts torn and broken. Lives rebuilt.

It seemed like so long ago until they gathered here today, players from multiple generations, looking to have fun and give back to the town they were raised in.

The Middletons grabbed seats on the low side of the bleachers, while the Shaw family filled a quarter-section on the opposite side. The Shoemaker girls stood at the field's edge, talking deliberately. Sporting notice-me-first fan attire, the girls made it a point to be in full view of any available single male on the premises, and with a baseball game about to get under way, there were plenty.

Robin passed them with a quick smile, drew up to Liv's side and gave her a quick half hug. "Doing all right?"

"I think we're going to do well," Liv admitted, eyeing the growing crowd, "and that's huge. Seeing the town succeed with these events makes me even more nostalgic about staying here."

"Have you forgiven him yet?" Robin aimed a glance in Jack's direction and burst out laughing at the telltale expression on Liv's face. "You have it bad, Livvie Franklin. I think the only good part of that is that he's as besotted as you are, and while that's cute as can be, us single girls might get a little green-eyed. Although after hearing about all that ranching stuff in detail…?" Robin made a face that said a life filled with birthing cattle didn't make her shortlist. "I'm okay being a townie."

Jack stepped up to the middle of the field, keyed the mike and drew the crowd's attention with a quick "Good morning."

"Mornin', Jack!" The Shoemaker girls waved as a unit, openly flirting with Liv's Jack. Except he *wasn't* hers, so she couldn't exactly march onto that field and stake a claim even the Shoemaker girls couldn't miss. Instead, she folded her arms, refused to glare in their direction and listened as Jack addressed the crowd.

He introduced the players from both teams. Some of the guys took a ribbing for being stouter than they used to be, but it was all in fun until Jack had Sonny haul out two boxes of uniform shirts. As the players lined up along the first-base and third-base sides, Sonny and Coach Randolph handed out the just-arrived Old-timers' "Player" shirts.

And when they had the shirts in hand on both sides of home plate, Jack held one aloft. "Today we want to join Major League Baseball in raising awareness of a rough disease, a disease that's affected several families in our town." He pointed out the deep purple ribbon on the left sleeve, then the Raising Alzheimer's Awareness logo on the right-hand sleeve. "As our population ages, it's good for us to become more aware of the signs and treatments available for folks struggling with Alzheimer's disease." He made eye contact with Liv but didn't lift his gaze to her grandfather or Lulu Jensen, showing the sensitivity she loved about him. He smiled at her and then the crowd in general. "The proceeds from these shirts will go to help research a cure for Alzheimer's. And the proceeds from your ticket sales and purchases today will help fund our new Jasper Gulch Historical Museum. Rusty?" He called the ninety-six-year-old off the bench, and handed him the ball. "Rusty Zidek, will you do us the honor of throwing the first pitch?"

Rusty's hand shook as he accepted the ball.

The crowd went still, all eyes on the aged man they knew so well. A man who exemplified the West, a cowboy, a wrangler, a sage and baseball player. It didn't get more all-American than Rusty Zidek, and the people of Jasper Gulch knew it. They stayed hushed and expectant, waiting while Rusty took a spot just in front of the pitcher's mound, wound up and threw.

A strike, dead-on.

The catcher caught the ball, sprang up and strode to the mound to congratulate Rusty. The old man's smile cragged a wealth of wrinkles beneath two shaggy brows and an overgrown handlebar mustache. "I say we get this game goin'!"

The crowd surged to its feet as the high school band marched forward to play an emotion-charged rendition of "The Star-Spangled Banner." In true baseball form, the fans anticipated the final notes and cheered the players, the day and the town in a show of hometown spirit that made Liv smile.

Robin was right. Jasper Gulch *was* special; she hadn't valued that the way she should have. God and good strong parents had given her room to spread her wings while staying quietly rooted to her hometown.

She might not have treasured that as a younger woman. Now? She understood more, much more.

The game began, a heated battle of strong pitching and well-placed batting. She watched the game but kept her eye on Jack. Would he be all right? Could he handle being back on the field, in front of the crowds, knowing his dream was gone forever? She'd learned the hard way that even old dreams packed a punch, a two-edged sword of reality.

Jack paced the Jasper Gulch Bobcats team dugout, jaw tight, eyes on the field. When he wasn't pacing, he was standing, staring straight out, clenching the rail in front of him. Her heart went out to him, despite years of spurning baseball. She'd blamed him and the sport, avoiding both, much as Jack had done. Seeing him, watching the tension darken his gaze, narrow his eyes…

No matter what happened…or didn't happen… between them, she wanted him happy.

The game rolled on, tight and tied with a score of 2–2, right up until the end of the fifth inning when a shout from the stands drew the attention of the Bobcat approaching the batter's box.

"Hey, Ben! I'm afraid you're going to miss this at bat." The very pregnant woman in the stands made a face that said no words were necessary.

"Now?" The thirtysomething outfielder looked at her, then the bat as if weighing his options, and he might have looked at the bat longer if Jack hadn't stepped to the plate and taken it out of his hands.

"Call me later, tell me if it's a boy or a girl."

Reason seemed to grab hold of Ben once Jack took the bat, and the expectant father bounded across the grass to the bleachers while Sam Douglas and his wife helped the laboring woman down.

Jack turned as if about to call someone off the bench, but there was no one to call. The sight of him there, in the batter's box, ready to hit, pushed Liv to action. She didn't pause to consider the outcome, good or bad. She didn't weigh up how her action might affect the man she loved, she simply knew that Jack was right where he belonged, at long last. Standing at home plate, bat in hand, squared up in the batter's box.

She moved forward, rallying the crowd, fist-pumping the air. "We want Jack! We want Jack! We want Jack!"

The crowd didn't waste a moment. Within seconds, both bleachers were on their feet, cheering and waving Jasper Gulch banners, shouting Jack's name.

He turned. Looked at Liv. And the look she saw on his face, in his gaze, said that despite years of misgiving, he'd never forget this moment, a moment she gave him.

She smiled, fist-pumped the air, jerked her head toward home plate and mouthed, "Go get 'em."

When the first pitch sailed in for a fastball strike down the center, Jack eyed the ball, then his bat as if reacquainting himself. The second ball arced away from him, a called "ball." The third pitch, a cutter, came dead-on then dived low, but did that stop Jack McGuire?

No way.

A low-ball hitter from way back, Jack dug down, swinging hard and fast, driving the ball with the quintessential crack of a home run.

The crowd went wild on both bleachers. Shouts of joy and cheers of laughter filled the park as Jack rounded the bases in his typical calm fashion, but when he crossed home plate, did he stay calm?

He did not!

With all the energy of an athlete at the top of his game, Jack ran to the field's edge, grabbed up Liv and kissed her soundly in front of nearly twelve hundred people.

And she kissed him right back, delighted and unafraid to stake her own personal claim on the tall, green-eyed rancher.

The crowd cheered again, and they didn't start to calm until Jack raised a hand in the air. It took a long moment for things to wind down, but when they did, Jack McGuire smiled and took a knee on the dusty ground.

The crowd's quiet gasp echoed Liv's.

"Liv, I've loved you a long time and I can't think of anything nicer or more wonderful than making you my wife, raisin' a family with you on the Double M. What do you think, Livvie Franklin? Will you do this cowboy the honor of becoming my wife?"

Would she?

Jack's sweet proposal required no thought, but he didn't know that. Livvie pretended to think the question over, playing the crowd, but in the end she met his gaze, the true-and-trusty smile of a born rancher, and nodded. "It would be my pleasure, cowboy."

Jack jumped up and kissed her again, and by the time they got the romance of the day settled, it was time to play ball again.

He trotted back onto the field, tall and strong, as if baseball was the only thing on his mind, while Liv's heart skip-jumped in her chest. Thoughts of what could be filled her head—the ranch, a home, a house full of little McGuires. She couldn't be happier, and a glance up to her parents said she had their full approval. Grandma fist-pumped the air and Mert's grin from the third-base bleachers said she had them pegged right all along.

The game ended four innings later with the Senior Bobcats losing by one to the Senior Bombers, but no one cared. As the afternoon of fun wore on, the entire town seemed energized by the success of the day. Happy smiles and joyous high fives were the norm along Main Street and the ball fields.

And when Jack approached Liv's family after the game, he made a face of apology to her father. "I should have asked you first, sir."

"You did," Dave replied. "Ten years ago. Woulda answered the same now as then."

Jack slung an arm around Liv, drew her close and planted a kiss to her right temple as Grandma and Grandpa drew closer.

"That was some game, young man!" The old man gripped the cane in his right hand and gave it a notable *thump!* "Half the time I didn't know who was winning or who was playing for who, but it didn't matter. I haven't been to a ball game that good in years, although I don't know about purple shirts and ribbons for ballplayers." His face said someone had gone astray, sissifying the players' shirts like that.

Jack met the old man's gaze. "I can't imagine what they were thinking, sir."

He'd said just the right thing. The old man's smile accepted the words, and as Grandma Mason hugged Grandpa's arm, Liv knew that's how she wanted to spend her days, all of her days. For better or worse, in sickness and in health…

From this day forward.

Epilogue

❧

"Carrie, are you really making a basket for the country fair?" Liv aimed a teasing look toward Mick and Jack as they worked to replace the shed roof abutting the near barn in early September. "I thought once we caught the guy, we could ignore things like that."

"It does negate the point, doesn't it?" Carrie laughed when Mick aimed an amused look from his vantage point on the roof. "Mick would just as soon stay out here and work, so I'm making one to encourage his presence. If he doesn't come to town, I'll be having lunch with some other spit-shined cowboy that day."

"That's not likely to happen," Jack called down as he finished the final corner along the drip edge. "I've been instructed to outbid anyone who bids on your basket if Dad's tied up here."

"Mick McGuire!" Carrie leaned back on her arms and laughed up at Jack's father while Livvie turned the potatoes roasting in the fire-pit coals. "That's kind of romantic, you staking a claim and all."

"I think that rock on your hand oughta be claim enough, but just in case one of those youngsters gets an idea in his head, I made sure Jack's got things covered."

"Like father like son," Liv muttered just loud enough for Carrie to hear. "Apple didn't fall far from the tree in this case, and you know what?"

Carrie hiked one eyebrow, waiting.

"I'd say that's all right and we're the two most blessed women in Jasper Gulch right now."

"I can't disagree, although that house is going to be a mite crowded come spring."

"No, it won't." Jack swung off the roof and landed solid, looking just as good nailing shingles as he did riding herd, and Jack McGuire looked mighty fine on the back of a horse. "Liv and I saw Ben over at the lumber works. We were going to wait until spring, but I decided there's no time like the present to start the new house. If we get the outside up and weather-tight before the snow hits, we're golden. That would have us in before calving season."

"Having that twenty-thousand-dollar check clear the bank a few weeks back made the prospect of building more manageable."

Jack stared at his father. "You knew about that?"

"Ayuh. I saw the transfer from your account online. And figured I'd watch and see how you handled things, and you did just fine. After going a little stupid for a few days. But I figured a few days was way better than a bunch of years, so let me just say—" Mick raised his hammer in salute "—you've gotten better, son."

Liv cleared her throat.

Carrie laughed.

"It seems the bank had applied Henry's funds to someone else's account," Jack explained. "So when the bank bounced our check, they sent Henry a notice and he stormed into the bank ready to do battle because he figured we'd been denied our money. He called me personally to apologize the night of the Old-timers' Baseball Game."

"Wilbur said he felt bad, calling you, giving you the news," Mick added. "But in business, things happen. Best we can do is move on."

The kids came bounding from the house wearing hoodies and sweatpants, the cooler nights a reminder of a new time, a new season. "Mom, is the food ready yet?"

"Liv, I'm starving!"

They raced toward them, two faces, smiling, hungry and absolutely adorable. Blue followed right along, a four-legged bundle of happy energy, as cute and ravenous as his masters.

She'd gone from the prospect of being an assistant professor to an about-to-be-married woman, surrounded by cattle, horses, jobs, tasks, kids, dogs and a new family, filled with faith, hope and love.

Jack caught her eye from across the fire and his expression said he was just as delighted and amazed. And the thought of being here, with Jack, in their new home under the banquet of Big Sky country stars?

Made Livvie Franklin the happiest woman in the world.

* * * * *

If you liked this BIG SKY CENTENNIAL *novel,
watch for the next book,
HER MONTANA TWINS by Carolyne Aarsen,
available September 2014.*

And don't miss a single story in the
BIG SKY CENTENNIAL *miniseries:*

*Book #1: HER MONTANA COWBOY
by Valerie Hansen*

*Book #2: HIS MONTANA SWEETHEART
by Ruth Logan Herne*

*Book #3: HER MONTANA TWINS
by Carolyne Aarsen*

*Book #4: HIS MONTANA BRIDE
by Brenda Minton*

*Book #5: HIS MONTANA HOMECOMING
by Jenna Mindel*

*Book #6: HER MONTANA CHRISTMAS
by Arlene James*

Dear Reader,

Our God is the God of second chances. Sometimes they come unexpectedly, the silver lining within a cloud of regret.

Livvie's story struck home. I can see a young woman, denied the relationship she thought she'd have, working to rebuild her life according to plan. And how devastating it must feel when that plan runs amok! But it wasn't coincidence that brought her home at this time, or brought her grandfather's condition to light. God's timing isn't always convenient, but if we grab the offered opportunities, it's amazing how things work out.

And Jack? Denied the career he worked for, then losing his mother, he came back home to an amazing heritage. But it took him a while to shake off that anger, the yearning for control.

We're such funny creatures. We want to take charge, but we forget that not everything is in our control. For me, that's when the Serenity Prayer grabs hold. "Dear Lord, Grant me the courage to change the things I can, the patience to accept the things I cannot change and the wisdom to know the difference." Simple words. Beautiful guidelines!

I lost my father-in-law to Alzheimer's in 2012 after a long, debilitating illness. It was heartbreaking to see this kindly man suffer the indignities of a mind-numbing disease, but you know what? His family rose to the occasion and became my models for the Franklins in this book. Seeing my mother-in-law's dedicated care, we glimpsed her strength and faith firsthand.

I enjoyed writing this story, delving into Big Sky country! I love hearing from readers. Contact me at *ruthy@ruthloganherne.com,* friend me on Facebook at Ruth Logan Herne, come cook with me at www.yankeebellecafe.blogspot.com and access my website, *ruthloganherne.com.* I enjoy chatting with folks, sharing stories and prayers! God bless you and thanks so much for reading *His Montana Sweetheart!*

Ruthy

Questions for Discussion

1. Coming "home" isn't always easy. For some it's a walk down memory lane. For others, it's more like walking the plank. Are there people in your family who might cringe at coming home? What can we do to ease their return?

2. When his college injury made Major League Baseball an impossible dream, Jack shrugged off everything that might remind him of the dream he lost, including Olivia. Have you ever made a "thing" or goal so important that it blinded you to the worthiness of the rest of your life?

3. Jack believes in God but isn't sure what role God really plays in life. The new preacher's words touch Jack's heart and bring him closer to the roots of his faith. Ethan's arrival in town, the centennial celebrations and Liv's return all coincide to bring Jack to his destiny. Do you believe in God's timing? Has it manifested itself in your life?

4. Liv embraced a lifestyle just as segregated as Jack's. She rarely visited home, she didn't see her grandparents, and immersed herself in her own life and work. Her grandfather's worsen-

ing battle with Alzheimer's is a wake-up call for Livvie. Guilt reminds her that a selfish existence is really no existence at all. Do you think that guilt can be a helpful tool, guiding us to become better people?

5. Adopting the neglected horse is a big step forward for Livvie and Jack. She'll need to come to the ranch—a place rife with memories, a place she loves—to take care of Dilly. Her commitment gives her the excuse she's longing for, a chance to be with Jack again, on the ranch. Do you say yes to the possibilities life offers often enough? Or do you let apprehension steer you away?

6. Jasper Gulch is its own conundrum. Some folks want to move forward while some cling to the past, avoiding change purposely. In a small town, this can become a harsh duel. What methods would you recommend to entice a town to work together? And do you think the centennial celebrations might help do just that?

7. Jack's father is falling in love. And if that happiness includes a new wife and two cute fatherless kids, Jack sees that as a triple win. But when Jack thinks he messed things up, his guilt is magnified. It's not just him and his father

anymore, and that raises the stakes. Does added responsibility make us hesitate to take chances? Is that a good thing?

8. The arrival of Liv's grandparents changes her family dynamic. Then, when Liv sees her lack of time investment in the past, she's realizing her choices weren't made of faith and emotion but convenience. Her grandmother's wisdom reminds her that everyone has regrets on the path of life. What's the best way to push beyond those old regrets into a new tomorrow?

9. Grandma's not happy with the turns her life has taken, but when she withdraws a beautiful piece, created for an event that no longer existed, the knitters see beyond her snippiness. Her words paint a picture of a life changed, through no fault of her own, and their sympathy takes hold. How can we be helpful to people dealing with the trauma of aging and disease?

10. Liv is ready and willing to make a commitment to Jack and Jasper Gulch, but when Jack pulls back, she's reminded of their broken dreams from college. The growth of her faith has helped her to see her own part in the problems. Jack's actions spawn Liv's reaction and she's not afraid to give Jack a wake-up call.

Does your faith in God help you to be honest in your relationships?

11. When Jack reveals the "team" shirts he ordered, with a ribbon marking Alzheimer's awareness, Liv's heart is touched. Jack's respect for the elderly makes Liv realize how much she loves him. His action reflects the love and respect her grandmother shows her ailing grandfather, the kind of love that lasts a lifetime. Do you have examples of this kind of love in your family? If not, how do you grasp hold of your own personal "happily ever after"?

LARGER-PRINT BOOKS!

GET 2 FREE
LARGER-PRINT NOVELS
PLUS 2 FREE
MYSTERY GIFTS

Love Inspired®
SUSPENSE
RIVETING INSPIRATIONAL ROMANCE

Larger-print novels are now available...

ReaderService.com

Manage your account online!

- Review your order history
- Manage your payments
- Update your address

*We've designed
the Harlequin® Reader Service
website just for you.*

Enjoy all the features!

- Reader excerpts from any series
- Respond to mailings and special monthly offers
- Discover new series available to you
- Browse the Bonus Bucks catalog
- Share your feedback

Visit us at:

ReaderService.com